ROMANCE

Large Print Vog
Vogt, Esther Loewen.
The flame and the fury

The Flame

and the

Fury

*Also by Esther Vogt
in Large Print:*

Song of the Prairie
Edge of Dawn

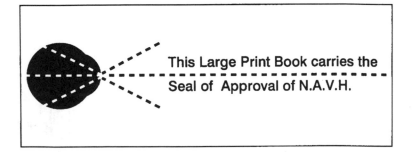

This Large Print Book carries the
Seal of Approval of N.A.V.H.

The Flame

and the

Fury

Esther Vogt

Thorndike Press • Thorndike, Maine

All Scripture taken from the Holy Bible:
King James Version.

Published in 2000 by arrangement with Christian Publications.

Thorndike Press Large Print Candlelight Series.

The tree indicium is a trademark of Thorndike Press.

The text of this Large Print edition is unabridged.
Other aspects of the book may vary from the original edition.

Set in 16 pt. Plantin by Elena Picard.

Printed in the United States on permanent paper.

Library of Congress Cataloging-in-Publication Data

Vogt, Esther Loewen.
   The flame and the fury / Esther Vogt.
      p. cm.
   ISBN 0-7862-2796-6 (lg. print : hc : alk. paper)
   1. Kansas — History — Civil War, 1861–1865 — Fiction.
   2. Quantrill, William Clarke, 1837–1865 — Fiction.
   3. Massacres — Fiction. 4. Large type books. I. Title.
   PS3572.O3 F57 2000
      813'.54—dc21   00-042572

DEDICATION

To my dear friend and neighbor, Rosemary Freeman, who has been a steady friend and encourager through the years I have known her. We've laughed together, prayed together; we have shared hopes and dreams, phone calls and lives. She's been such a special friend! I dedicate this novel to her and also to her lovely family. God bless them all!

"When thou passest through the waters, I will be with thee; and through the rivers, they shall not overflow thee: when thou walkest through the fire, thou shalt not be burned; neither shall the flame kindle upon thee. For I am the LORD thy God, the Holy One of Israel, thy Saviour. . . . Fear not: for I am with thee." (Isaiah 43:2–3, 5)

AUTHOR'S NOTE

The long line of men following William Clark Quantrill that fateful morning of Friday, August 21, 1863 were edgy as they neared Lawrence.

When the raiders entered the town near 11th and Rhode Island Streets, they realized they had achieved total surprise of their free-state enemies. Oh, yes, the town had been warned, but who would believe anyone would be so cruel, so foolish, to attack the town simply because it was a hotbed for free-staters and housed black fugitives? The Massachusetts Aid Society for Emigrants to Kansas had already set up steam sawmills and a grist mill and had established newspapers in Lawrence because it was a stronghold for free-state causes.

Kansas did not become a state until January 29, 1861. In 1854 the Kansas-Nebraska Act allowed the issue of slavery to be settled by popular sovereignty in the territories of Kansas and Nebraska. After the votes were counted, it was the free-state faction that won in Kansas, although the Missourians and other proslavery people insisted that it must become a slave state "to preserve the Union." Some became violently angry when this didn't happen and much bad feeling erupted.

William Clark Quantrill was determined, with his band of 294 raiders, or "bushwhackers," to "punish" Lawrence with its strong free-state sentiments for the results of the vote. He made a list of men from Lawrence that he wanted to have killed, and that morning his raiders stole silently on the sleeping town to do just that and then leave the town in smoldering ruins.

The chief person targeted on the list was U.S. Senator Jim Lane. Fortunately, Lane escaped, but at least 150 or more others were left dead. Curiously, many of the men marked for death on Quantrill's list escaped.

After the town was torched, fully half of the homes in Lawrence were reduced to ashes. (This is the background in which the Davis family, fictitious characters of the story, experience this tragic event.) But the valiant people of Lawrence, after a time of grieving and sorrow, rebuilt the town into a thriving city, known for Kansas' largest university (University of Kansas) built on Mount Oread.

Although Quantrill and his band escaped, he met his death later in Kentucky at age twenty-seven.

Relive that horrendous event and its aftermath in the story of *The Flame and the Fury*. The main events are fully factual, a portion of actual Kansas history.

Esther Loewen Vogt

Chapter 1

Stepping cautiously down the narrow path that crawled amid a clutter of rocks toward the ravine from the frame cottage, Beth Davis walked slowly through the dip in the western end of town. She paused and looked around. The bright May afternoon of 1863 had grown warm. She stopped, drew off her yellow-checked sunbonnet, shook out her light brown hair and fanned her face.

Lawrence, the small town in the northeast part of the state of Kansas, drowsed sleepily in the sunshine, and she drew a deep, satisfying breath. What magnificent country! The virgin prairie to the west rolled across the stretching plains of daisy-starred verdure and softened into hills of lavender mist.

Beth, her father Ben and her nine-year-old brother Andy had arrived the year before. An associate of her father had persuaded Ben and his family to leave their home in Massachusetts for this raw new territory to help build it into a state as a part of the antislavery cause. Kansas had become a state on January 29, 1861, over two years before. Although the town's population boasted only around 2,000, stragglers were arriving almost daily in creaking covered wagons loaded with possessions. It was becoming a fine town with comfortable homes and wide streets, bustling with businesses along wide Massachusetts Street, which stretched north and south.

Beth smiled, knowing that the question of whether the state would be "free" or "slave" had been settled satisfactorily, although by a small margin. Antislavery advocates had worked hard to populate Kansas with free-state people, and their plan had worked well enough to make Kansas free.

She gazed across the dim outlines of the hills to the west, then twisted her slim body to the northeast where the Kansas River lapped at its banks in the bright afternoon sun.

"This is gonna become a good state, albeit a troubled one," her father had said when they had arrived in early March of 1862, his beard bristling.

"But President Lincoln has signed the bill making this state free and joining it with the Union," Beth had added in a firm voice. "So why should the state still face trouble?"

Ben Davis had twirled his brown and gray

handlebar mustache with long, thin fingers. "There's been rumors. . . ." His words trailed away.

"Rumors? What kind of rumors, Pa?"

"Ya know — bushwhackers who wanted to make Kansas a slave state. They ain't forgiven us free-staters for messin' up their plans to turn Kansas into a part of the Confederacy."

Well, whatever lies ahead, she thought this cheery May day, *surely the Lord is in charge, for right has prevailed at last.*

She paused along the path, then turned her footsteps up the slope toward the dusty streets of Lawrence. In the distance where the Kansas River bordered the town, she could make out the dim shape of the gristmill where Pa worked. The millstones had come from France with the rocks quarried locally to build its strong foundation. There were two buhrstones — one for wheat and one for corn, Pa had said. Piles of grain were already stored on the ground in several bins behind the mill.

Just then she saw a hurrying figure approaching along the trail from town, and she beamed as she recognized her best friend. Beth rushed to meet the slight, dark-haired figure.

"Dorie Campbell!" she cried. "How did

you know where to find me? I took off without telling anyone."

Dorie's laugh was a merry tinkle. "Oh, your brother said he'd seen you hiking down the ravine when I found him at the house chewing on an apple."

"Andy? I didn't know he knew I left. That boy's never around when I need him to fill the woodbox or fetch kindling for the cookstove or a pail of water. But I'm glad he was home for a change."

"He said you were probably heading out toward Dan Wilcox's place — and when I looked west I saw you trotting back up the trail. Tell me, did you find Dan at home?"

"Of course not." She frowned. "But Andy somehow has it stuck in his head that I should be interested in that young farmer." Beth snorted. "Why, I'll never know."

Dorie linked her slender arm through Beth's as they ambled back into town.

"You *should* know! Dan Wilcox is just about the handsomest man around. Believe me, he likes you. Besides, you're eighteen, Beth, and you should start thinking about romance."

Beth stopped short and wrinkled her pert nose. "I'm not so sure I'm that fond of him."

"Why not? He's generally all-around gallant and jolly, and you'd make a handsome

14

pair," Dorie said brightly. "What do you have against him?"

"I — can't put my finger on it. I guess I'm not ready to leave Pa and Andy and marry the first young man who makes sheep's eyes at me!" Beth flared, starting up the slope. "What about you?"

"I've decided to set my cap for Ed Wallace. He's walked me home from church a time or two, and my folks think he'd make a fine husband. He's always doing things for the church and his voice really carries the bass section in the choir, clear up to the rafters. But you could do a lot worse than Dan Wilcox, you know."

"Maybe so, but Dan seldom comes to church. That's one reason I've hesitated."

The Plymouth Congregational Church was growing. No doubt Pastor Richard Cordley had a good new helper in Lynn Nelson, assisting wherever he could. Beth had heard that Lynn had a passion for the young people. But Dan rarely joined his friends there. Besides, there were other young men in Lawrence. Why should she hurry?

Dorie loosed her arm and paused on the street corner, smoothing her crisp blue gingham skirt with its fichu of lace around the collar. "I must be going, Beth. I promised Mother I'd help her with the evening meal, especially since she hurt her leg crossing the ravine yesterday." She paused. "Will I see you at Mrs. Robinson's quilting tomorrow?"

Beth paused and eyed her friend. "I'll really try. I have so much to do. Since my mother's gone —" her voice broke.

Dorie turned to hug her friend. "It must be hard, losing your mother, way off in Massachusetts. And you don't have an easy time looking after your lively brother!"

"Such a rapscallion nine-year-old isn't easy to handle," Beth said as Dorie headed up the slope. Beth watched until Dorie disappeared around the bend.

Andy really wasn't a bad boy, Beth mused; he was just so independent and went his own way too often without telling her where he was going. But the town was free and easygoing and so were the youngsters.

Already the sun slipped toward the west. A small breeze had sprung up, and the scent of wild roses wafted over the prairie as she headed toward the house. It was time she thought of fixing supper. There would be fried potatoes with generous slices of green onion — if she had time to fix them.

"Good afternoon, Beth," a cheerful voice called to her as the clip-clop of a horse sounded behind her. Dan Wilcox. She stopped short and sighed. Certainly Dan was handsome — and debonair — and sitting in the saddle of his roan he made a dashing figure. His hair was the sandy color of the soil in the ravine, and his dark-blue eyes danced with eagerness. Beth's smile was tight. *He tries too hard to be charming,* she told herself.

"Well, how're things with you up here on the edge of town?" he said, relaxing in his saddle as she walked toward the small white frame cottage near the ravine path.

"About as usual, I suppose," she said lightly. "I'm late getting back to fix supper. Pa will be home soon. And it's hard to tell where Andy is skulking around today!"

"As long as he doesn't wander too far from the outskirts of town. There's a lot of uneasy talk, especially now that Charley Hart's been seen lurking in the area."

Beth bristled. "Why does everyone think Charley's a troublemaker? I've met him several times and I thought he was quite likable — a sort of quiet, gentle person. People seem to have it in for him — all the talk you hear about him!"

"I'm not so sure, Beth. He's been accused of horse stealing and a few other things."

"Well, some folks let off steam by being

ornery, and some just avoid going to church!" she said tartly.

"Are you saying that because I haven't been to church much lately it makes me a sort of hoodlum too?" Dan chuckled.

"I didn't say —"

"I'm no Charley Hart! Besides, I'm trying to prove up my claim. Being five miles from town has kept me at home plenty of times to deliver a calf or some other emergency!"

"That's your business!" she said primly. "Still — I don't think Charley will be a problem like everyone seems to think. He's being looked down upon. He doesn't have any parents, and there's no one to show him a better way. Doesn't the Bible say to turn the other cheek — to show compassion? He seemed most pleasant and charming when I met him, so don't be too hard on the poor fellow."

Dan slid from his horse and turned to her angrily. "I hope you're right. But that isn't what Jim Lane says!"

"Jim Lane's reputation hasn't been too savory either! Remember how he and some of his militia have tried to rout the Missouri farmers along the Kansas border!"

"That's because Jim makes it his job to look after everybody in town. Oh, Beth, I don't want to quarrel with you, but please

18

be careful! Rumors are that Charley Hart's angry with Lawrence — for some dumb reason!"

She turned abruptly, hurried into the kitchen and slammed the door. Through the window she watched Dan mount his saddle and ride away. Why did Dan have to believe Hart was bent on making trouble? Well, Charley could have changed — some claimed he'd even called himself William Clark Quantrill. What a classy name! After all, the man had some education and had even taught school at Stanton for some time. But few people seemed impressed.

Well, she wasn't interested in men now. Helping Brother Cordley in church and being concerned about making a home for Pa and Andy took her time.

She took the skillet from its nail on the wall and began to peel potatoes.

Chapter 2

Nearly every day new immigrants moved to the antislavery town of Lawrence, home to avid free-stater James Lane. While active in the Union Army, Jim Lane had at one time served as a senator in Washington and helped protect President Lincoln at the White House when his life was threatened.

The partisan conflict going on in territorial Kansas was typical of severe disagreements that led to the Civil War. In 1854 the Kansas-Nebraska Act was passed, which allowed the issue of slavery to be settled by popular sovereignty in Kansas and Nebraska. This act caused many ill feelings in the North because earlier compromises on the spread of slavery became null upon the Act's passage into law. No wonder both proslavery and antislavery groups rushed to fill Kansas with settlers of their own sentiments — communities loyal to one side or another. Obviously Lawrence had become one of the strongest antislavery settlements in Kansas.

Lawrence had grown into a substantial

little city of over 2,000 citizens. Its wide main street led north toward the Kansas River. There were over seventy businesses and well-built homes, most constructed of wood or stone-quarried rock. Half a dozen churches were scattered throughout the town.

If one climbed Mount Oread, to the southwest of the town, a pleasant view of the prairie and fields to the west was the reward. To the northeast of the mount, a deep ravine meandered through town, dividing northern Lawrence neatly in half. Low bridges spanned the chasm here and there, and spreading trees lined its banks.

In the north corner of the ravine, in Central Park, lived Reverend Hugh Fisher, who had been a chaplain for James Lane, and his family in his fine brick home. Near the river lay the shantytown of nearly a thousand blacks, former slaves.

But politics riddled with foul play resulted in violence. In 1856 proslavery raiders burned a part of the town, and in retaliation John Brown and his men massacred five allegedly proslavery citizens. By 1857, the population in Kansas had increased to allow the territory to apply for statehood. Although proslavery forces were in the minority, they had gathered enough support to approve a proslavery constitution. But in a new election antislavery forces won.

Yet the political climate in Washington prevented Kansas from being admitted to the Union until early 1861 after many Southerners in Congress resigned as a result of their states' secession from the Union. Still, the loss of Kansas to the antislavery side rankled many Southerners, especially those from Missouri and Texas.

The papers were full of reports on angry proslavery men like William Clark Quantrill, who went under an alias of Charley Hart. He had lived in Lawrence now and then after teaching school at Stanton but spent time with the Delaware Indians on the reservation north of the river. Few persons realized what his real name was.

While living in Lawrence, he had been both a border ruffian (proslavery) and jayhawker (antislavery). Border ruffians loitered along the ferry landing and played both sides of the issue for all they could get from it.

After the Civil War began, Western Missouri was greatly affected by the struggle. People on both sides were attacked and murdered. James Lane was known to attack some areas in Missouri where he pillaged stores and looted homes. No wonder some folks hated James Lane. Kansas had formed a militia to protect Kansans from the border ruffians, and Lane had been made the general of the Kansas militia.

All this turmoil was bound to produce military action. A scout was sent to check out these rumors about Quantrill — but found nothing.

But Quantrill had secretly sent spies to Lawrence. Charles T. "Fletch" Taylor, who was sent to Lawrence under the pretext of speculating on a claim, lodged at the Eldridge House hotel and seemed most friendly and agreeable. This was where things stood in June 1863.

When Ben Davis came home from the mill he was full of talk. "Them rumors is rollin' thick and fast," he said, pulling off his sweat-stained hat, speckled with chaff and straw. "Folks is really suspectin' Charley Hart's behind much of the unrest, but nobody can prove nothin'."

Beth scooped a skilletful of buttered dried corn into a bowl and set a plate of fresh-baked wheat bread on the table. She pressed her lips together firmly. "Here we go again, blaming Charley without cause. I think it's stupid to think he's the one at fault without proof."

Pa hung up the towel after washing his face and hands. "Yeah, that's how it looks, but he's hinted at things no one has bothered to check out, they say."

"We have our armory and most of the men in town have their own guns," Beth flared. "That should offer some protection if Lawrence needs it — which I seriously doubt. Besides, there are two camps outside town with Kansas militia, one of former slaves."

Just then Andy slammed into the kitchen and slid into his chair by the table.

"Here, here, Andy," Beth ordered. "Get washed up first if you want to eat!"

Pa sat down at the table. "We can't always count on the militia. Mayor Collamore has ordered all men with a musket or pistol to donate it to the armory. What good will that do if we're attacked?"

"Have you taken your musket, Pa?" Beth's face blanched.

"Them's the mayor's orders."

Andy splashed his face in the washbasin and gave it a few quick swipes with the towel. "Does it mean us boys have to give up our slingshots too?" Andy grumbled as he slid into a chair with a frown on his freckled face.

Pa and Beth looked at each other and

smiled. "Well, maybe not your slingshot exactly," Pa said lightly. "There's still plenty of rocks around, but keep your ammunition dry."

After Pa's table prayer they ate in silence. *Are things becoming so desperate that even children's toys are confiscated?* Beth thought. *Lord, please don't let it come to that,* she prayed. *And don't let violence disrupt our peaceful town.* It was still inconceivable that Charley Hart — or whatever he called himself now — was accused of things rumored. Especially without proof. Besides, he came and went. No one seemed to know where he was from one day to the next.

After their meal, daylight was gone and dusk bore down slowly over the town in a dim, misty haze. Beth hung up the dish towel and walked into her tiny bedroom with its bed of oak, covered with a brightly pieced quilt, and lit the oil lamp. Mama had made the quilt some months before she had died four years ago, and gay scraps of colored percale and squares of blue gingham caught the glow of the yellow prairie moon shining through the window. Now she pulled the shade and undressed for bed. She had listened to Andy's prayers before he crawled into his cot in Pa's room, something he had done at Mama's knee when she was alive. The task of mothering her young brother had fallen on Beth.

As usual, she read a few verses of Scripture before she blew out the lamp and pulled the light quilt over her. The room had been stifling with the day's heat but had cooled as night fell.

She closed her eyes and tried to sleep, but the day's events crowded into her mind. It wasn't easy to fall asleep, thinking about the talk that Lawrence might be attacked. She pushed away all thoughts of evil men skulking in dark corners, waiting to do away with free-staters.

She had promised to go to the Plymouth Congregational Church in the morning to work on Mrs. Robinson's freshly pieced quilt. Mrs. Robinson's husband was the former governor, and they owned a lovely new home in town and were solid members of the church congregation. The conversation around the quilt would almost certainly be the job of finishing the drafty stone church. After all, the congregation had grown to seventy members, even though the pews were still mere planks laid on nail kegs. What they needed were real pews! In past winters they had huddled around the pot-bellied stove. Wind and snow gusted through the cracks, and it was time for the congregation to complete the church so important decisions could be made under a snug roof. With the thought of a warm, cozy church, Beth dropped off to sleep.

Bright morning sun dappled the floor with a mosaic of light and shadows when Beth got up. After cleaning up breakfast and picking the season's first green beans from their little garden, she hurried into her second-best dress of sturdy blue cotton and headed for the door. Pa had been off to work at the gristmill an hour ago, and Andy lolled in the doorway, eyeing the ravine through the open door with a frown. Beth turned to him.

"Andy, I'm going to church to work on Mrs. Robinson's quilt, but I must ask you to stay around the yard."

"Oh, Beth," he whined, "there ain't much to do here. I was at the ravine yesterday. I thought I'd go downtown today and watch the blacksmith shoe horses. Or to the livery stable and talk to the hands there. What's wrong with that?"

She pressed her lips into a firm line. "I don't want you roaming all over town. You know the saloons are full of drunks and sometimes they get rough."

"I'll keep away from 'em. I ain't a baby anymore!" His freckled face drew into a grimace.

"I know you're not. But — well, why don't you watch the workers finish up the trim on the Eldridge House? After all, it's said to be the finest hotel on the prairies, and it is gorgeous."

He grimaced and muttered. "Aw — all right, Beth. I'll be back in time for lunch." He grabbed his gray cap from its nail behind the kitchen door and slammed out of the house.

Beth put on her bonnet and left for church. It wasn't easy to keep one eye on her younger brother and still be involved in her own activities.

Hurrying down the dusty streets she soon reached the stone church that already swarmed with women and girls. A few carried babies on their hips as they made their way to the corner of the church where Mrs. Robinson's quilt was set up.

Myra Bates waved at Beth from her place in front of the brightly pieced coverlet. "So you made it, Beth. Come sit here by me and help me thread needles. I need your company! It seems like one dodges rumors on every corner. And most of them ain't too pleasant."

"You're referrin' to Charley Hart, no doubt," Millie Dixon chirped. "People seem to think he's not to be trusted. But he's still green and folks seem to have it in for him."

"That's what you think!" Myra snorted. "He ain't to be trusted, if you ask me. I'll never forget how smart-cocky he was about stealing Jim Taylor's horse — then skedaddled when he was accused!"

Beth seated herself beside Myra at the quilt. "Let's leave that misguided boy alone and concentrate on the fund-raiser for the church. What shall we do to raise money? This church building's not fit to worship in, and if we don't raise some money soon to fix it up, we'll be in a real scrape. How about a box social?"

Several of the young matrons nodded with approval as busy needles flew over the quilt.

"The unspoken-for girls may have a chance to find beaux who've just moved to town," Dorie Campbell piped up. "Of course, if Beth plays her cards right, she'll land Dan Wilcox without raising her eyebrows."

"Dan Wilcox!" Millie Dixon yipped. "Why, that young swain's hardly come to church since he moved here."

"Ain't a handsomer feller in town," Myra smirked, snapping her thread and smoothing her stitches carefully. "But it's a chance to show him the love of God, by fixin' a tasty box supper for the poor boy."

With a smile Beth lowered her gaze to the quilt. "First we'll have to get him to come."

"How about Charley Hart? Is someone gonna invite him?" one of the other girls snickered.

"If we can find him! He's in and out of Lawrence, it seems. Well, if we schedule three weeks from today, he may be in town again," Beth said.

The women chattered and sewed through the morning. Finally Beth unsnapped her watch from the chain around her neck and got up. "I'd better go home and fix lunch for Pa and Andy. I hope my little brother hasn't gotten into trouble, the way he scrambles around town!"

She picked up her bonnet, pushed her chair aside and started for the door. How nice if they could finish the renovations for the church before the hot summer.

Then she hurried down the path that led to their little house near the ravine. Pa was already home when she arrived. There was no sign of Andy. Beth got the iron pot and began to cook the green beans she'd picked earlier. She chopped a few pieces of salt pork and added it to the vegetables. Then she looked up at Pa.

"Where's Andy? He promised to be home by lunch."

Pa was at the washbasin soaping his grimy hands. "I met him by the new Liberty Bell as I came from the mill. He'll be home shortly."

"That boy really gets around!" Beth remarked, setting the coffeepot on the front of the cookstove. "He takes the most devious routes home he can find!"

Pa's face broke into a grin. "I promised I'd tell you both the story of that bell, and he said he'd be here in a hurry."

Pa told Beth more about what had happened during his morning at the mill, and then Andy bounded through the back door.

"Here I am, Pa!" he panted, throwing his cap into the corner. "You kin tell us the story of that bell now!" he said, careening to the table.

"First you wash up, Andy," Beth ordered. "You look a sight."

After a struggle with the damp washcloth, Andy swung into his chair, his face still glistening where the towel had missed it.

Pa paused for prayer, then passed the bowl of beans.

"What's the story, Pa?" Andy prodded.

"That bell and clock was brought to town by a plucky free-stater, Little Billy Hughes, from Leavenworth to Lawrence. Volunteered to bring it to Lawrence by steamboat

31

for $30, and said he wanted to do the job alone. He put that 1,600-pound bell in a crate, packin' hay over it and alternatin' hay and dishes until the crate was full. On the outskirts of Leavenworth four armed men stopped him and demanded to know what was in the barrel."

"What did Billy say?" Andy cut in. "If it had been me . . ."

"He said, 'Dishes!' They dug through the hay down to the second layer and didn't find the bell, so they let him go. A few miles further down, riders on horseback demanded to know if he had the bell. He said he had only dishes."

" 'Don't give us any Yankee lie,' one man spat out, and after divin' through three layers of hay they gave up and turned back. When he reached Lawrence it was ferried across — and rung by the stroke of the blacksmith's hammer." His face beamed.

"But why didn't they want the bell brought to Lawrence?" Beth asked anxiously.

Pa shrugged. "Anythin' to pester the free-staters."

"Didja see what it said on the bell?" Andy insisted.

"It said, 'Blessed is the people that know the joyful sound: they shall walk, O LORD, in the light of thy countenance.' "

Beth's heart leaped. Surely these words from Psalm 89:15 were a sign. It meant God would preserve the people of Lawrence in spite of vicious rumors. What could anyone do against His Word?

Chapter 3

The night of the fund-raiser lay clear and still. Stars shone in the black skies like jewels, and an aroma of fresh-cut hay hung in the evening air. Beth dressed carefully in her pale pink lawn with its swirl of ruffles around the neckline and slipped on a pair of pearl earrings. She coiled her light brown hair at the nape of her neck, then hurried out the door, carrying her box of food.

The young man who had arrived in town to help Pastor Cordley waited outside to greet people. His blond hair curled crisply over his forehead and his green eyes twinkled when Beth started for the church door.

"Hello!" he said cheerfully. "I'm Lynn Nelson. Some folks call me the assistant pastor," he chuckled as he lifted Beth's hand to his lips. "And who are you? I don't think we've met."

Beth smiled. "I'm Beth Davis and — no, I guess we haven't met before. My father and brother Andy and I live over by the ravine in the west part of town. And if you don't know my lively nine-year-old brother, you're in for a surprise."

She noticed Dan Wilcox standing to one side, tall, lean and jaunty in a plaid shirt and beige trousers. He moved next to Beth and took her elbow.

"This is quite a special lady, Nelson," Dan said, giving Beth's arm a light squeeze. "Fresh from Massachusetts, she came out here to set a few hearts aflutter."

Beth winced and drew herself away sharply. Dan was obviously trying to show her off as someone special to him, and she didn't like it.

Already the church swarmed with people dressed in clean, crisply ironed clothes. Beth excused herself and carried her box of food to the table in the front to be auctioned off. She had worked on the contents of her supper all afternoon: fried prairie chicken, a gooey strawberry tart and several boiled eggs. Leaving her box of food on the table, she turned her attention to several young men chatting behind her.

"He's been loitering on the north side of the river again," Ted Hess said brusquely, "and I don't like it!"

"He's plain obnoxious," lanky George French muttered, "and hangs around the thugs who kidnap slaves and ship them to

Missouri to be ransomed by their owners."

"It's all talk and no substance," Ted growled. "Let's lay all rumors aside and enjoy ourselves tonight."

Beth heartily agreed. The screech of fiddles and twang of guitars and a harmonica or two sounded in the background. Beth knew there would be singing to capture the evening's interest. The subject of gossip was apparently Charley Hart, and she was sick of it all.

Amid their noise and laughter she made her way to one side, for the bidding was about to begin. It could be lively, and she wondered who — if anyone — would venture to bid on her gaily wrapped box. With the arrival of so many newcomers one never knew who might take a risk on hers. As she turned her head, she saw Dan's easy grin as he winked at her. She knew without a doubt that Dan was going to bid on her box, although she'd tried to hide it unobtrusively in the folds of her full skirt when she arrived. Well, there were other young men who looked interested, and she shot Dan a challenging glance.

Soon Pastor Cordley's deep bass voice called for attention. "Welcome to our box social tonight! Our lovely ladies have outdone themselves, fixing up their most delectable suppers. As you all know, we must fix our church before summer farmwork takes away too many of our men, so please make your bids generous. But first let's sing a verse or two from 'Bringing in the Sheaves'! — although we hope the 'sheaves' will include some good jingling of coins!"

After an off-key squeak, the fiddler gave a pitch, and in the spirit of gaiety the song began. Beth joined in her clear soprano and was soon drawn completely into the spirit of the evening.

"Bringing in the sheaves! Bringing in the sheaves! We shall come rejoicing, . . ."

After the song, laughter spilled everywhere as the pastor raised his hand for silence. "Time to begin the bidding." He picked up a plainly wrapped box and called out, "How much for this fine dinner of — I think I smell something delicious! Whoever brought it will share it with the person whose bid is the highest."

A few halfhearted bids came from the boys on the sidelines and the men who apparently weren't too impressed with the simple brown paper box. Finally it sold for $1. Beth felt sorry for whoever the girl was who had worked so hard on the contents.

The bids on the boxes decorated with

bright ribbons and curls picked up momentum and soon grew lively. Beth kept her eyes open for her own box she had covered with leftover wallpaper they had brought along from Massachusetts. Someday they hoped to complete their house with more stylish walls than most of the Lawrence homes had. However, she could never match the style of Eldridge House hotel and the Robinsons' fancy house on the hill.

Suddenly Beth was aware that Pastor Cordley was holding her box in one hand, punctuating the air with the other fist as he called for bids.

"How much am I offered for this very attractive box of food? You know Lawrence boasts some of the loveliest young ladies in the state — all of whom are excellent homemakers. How much? I thought I saw — oh, I won't give away the beautiful lady's name! But make the bid a high one, boys!"

"Ten dollars!" Dan Wilcox shouted, and almost immediately the price was raised by Lynn Nelson to $12.

The noise of bidding rose high and shrill as both young men tried to outbid each other. Beth was embarrassed. When the bids reached $25, someone guffawed. "Well, with bids like that we'll soon have all the money we need to fix the church!"

A slender, blue-eyed young man in a smart brown suit stepped into the circle and snatched the box in his hand.

"This box is mine," he spoke in a firm, soft voice. A hush fell over the room as he made his way to Beth's side. Suspense and anger grew thick. It was then that Beth realized the slim man was Charley Hart! Red color seeped into her face. She knew she must share the food with him later.

Oh, dear God, she thought, her face burning with consternation, *why does it have to be the young man who dominates everyone's conversation, and why does it have to be so public?* He swung next to Beth and herded her into one corner of the church as she tried to snub him. Tearing open the box she'd so carefully fixed, he held it out to her.

"I'm s'posed to eat it with you, Miss Davis," he began in his soft, husky voice, and took her arm possessively.

Beth jerked her arm away roughly.

"What's wrong, Miss Davis? Scared of me? Just because I'm called a robber and a thief doesn't mean you can't share supper with me! Well? Are you eating with me or not?"

Beth shrank away from him.

He flung a handful of coins on the table

and hissed, "You haven't heard the last of me!"

Beth felt faint. Why in the world would Charley Hart — if that was his name — want her box? And why should *her* name be paired with his in the gossip that would soon fly thick and fast? Had he heard that she had halfheartedly defended him in the rumors of the past weeks? She trembled at the thought. And what did he mean — she hadn't heard the last of him?

Her mouth felt full of cotton, and she turned and fled to the door toward the street. Someone grabbed her arm and brought her to a stop.

"I'm glad you got rid of that sly lizard," Dan said sternly. "None of us dared believe he had the nerve to barge into our affairs! Well, that's as unpredictable as Quantrill is."

Beth pried Dan's hands from her arms and began to sob. "I've never been so mortified and humiliated in my life!"

"I'm sorry, Beth. Since I was gypped from getting your lunchbox, maybe you and I could go to the Eldridge House for a bite. How about it?"

"No, Dan!" she flung out. "Just take me home! I feel aw-awful!" He put his arm around her shoulders as they started down the street, tears trickling down her cheeks. Dan murmured words of comfort as they went toward the ravine path in the darkening evening.

"Well, one thing is sure — he really has nerve. Just forget him, Beth. Just forget him. The town will make an end to his boasting one of these days. What did he say when you left?"

Beth shook her head. "He said — he said folks called him a robber and a thief. And that I hadn't seen the last of him! I — don't know . . ."

"Just keep away from him, Beth. Please."

They had crossed the street. Lamplight spilled from the windows when they reached the kitchen door. Pa was seated at the table reading *The Kansas Tribune*, and he looked up as Dan and Beth came in.

"You home already? I didn't expect you so soon."

Dan led Beth to a chair and lowered her gently into it. "Well, there was — some excitement. Charley Hart showed up and bought Beth's box — then tried to make her eat with him. Ungrateful creature! That fella's a bigger puzzle than ever."

"So I hear," Pa said, laying the paper aside. "Are you all right, Beth?"

Scrubbing her cheeks, Beth nodded.

"Did you know Mayor Collamore's askin' for a permanent military garrison from the governor to protect the town? Although about twenty men were sent, only fifteen showed up. Not much help and protection," Pa muttered, "especially if Lawrence should be attacked, as rumors have it! It's believed Charley Hart was caught for stealin' a horse, but he must've escaped."

"He was sly and sullen when the sheriff tried to arrest him," Dan fumed, leaning against the door. "In fact, General Ewing, one of Kansas' top military men, had actually received word that Lawrence was to be attacked, but the small force that investigated the rumor found nothing." Dan shook his head. "I hope that creep will leave Lawrence alone now. Don't you worry, Beth-girl. Somehow things will simmer down. Just don't trust that rat any farther than you can throw him."

Then he turned and quietly left the house.

The next several days things settled down, but Beth felt conspicuous about Charley's insolent treatment of her at the social and stayed at home. She was in no mood to see anyone, and she was so nervous that she jumped at every strange noise. She puttered in the yard and tried to clean the rooms of their small house. But nothing she did calmed her. Had she defended a ruthless man? She hated to think so.

On Wednesday when she heard a knock at the door, she opened it hesitantly. Dorie stood there, her crisp pink bonnet cocked slightly askew. Relief flooded through Beth.

"I decided you needed to get out and see something besides these four walls," Dorie said, pushing the bonnet back on her head. "So how about a walk out along the ravine? The prairies are so alive with foliage, and you need a breath of air. Grab your hat and let's head out to the west."

With a sigh, Beth donned her bonnet and followed Dorie outside. Andy had begged to go to the grove of elm trees and reluctantly Beth had given him permission.

High cauliflower clouds seemed to hang without movement in the blue sky, their curd-like bases in folded valleys cool and distant in the west. A heavy, warm somnolence hung over the valley. The Robinsons' house, when they passed it, was rimmed by tall, stiff hollyhocks that reared deep maroon, creamy heads from the neatly trimmed yard.

"So Dan Wilcox rescued you from that pernicious scum, Charley Hart," Dorie said after they had walked in silence for some minutes.

Beth hesitated. "Well . . . he didn't really rescue me. Dan is fun, clever and I do appreciate him, especially his walking me home from the social after — after what Charley — oh, Dorie, I don't know what to think! Dan is — well, he's really nice and seems to like me, and I don't know if I like him. Still —"

"But why not? He's started to come to church, hasn't he? And that's what you want, isn't it?"

Beth paused in the path and pushed her foot back and forth in the dust. "Y-yes, Dorie. But I'm just not ready to commit myself to anyone. Dan doesn't really seem to know the Lord in the way I'd hoped he would."

"Had Charley Hart seen you before that night? Or was it the first time at the box social?" Dorie pressed anxiously.

"I met him once or twice earlier. He was very polite and pleasant. Maybe I wasn't distrustful of him like many others. But I certainly don't want to get involved with him! Something about him makes me — shudder."

Dorie nodded. "He did embarrass you at the box social. But earlier you seemed to defend him. Maybe he got wind of that, and that's why he took a shine to you."

The two girls had walked nearly a mile across the hills that dipped and swelled in the late afternoon shadows. Beth was lost in thought. "What do you think of the whole situation, Dorie?"

"I — don't know, Beth. You know Dan likes you. But he will also wonder if Charley Hart — or whatever his name is — may have further designs on you, especially after what he said. If you had to make a choice between Dan and Charley, who would it be?"

Beth stopped short, stunned at Dorie's blunt words. "Oh, Dorie! How can you think for one moment — as if I needed to make a choice!" she flared. "It hasn't come to that, has it?" she flung out. "He — bought my box but I refused to share it with him. I only hope that's the end of it!"

Dorie took her arm. "Let's head back home. I guess we were both a little silly and got carried away with all the rumors. I just don't want you to get involved with that Charley, especially after what he said — that you hadn't seen the last of him. That man can be as charming as a snake. I hope you'll avoid him." Dorie paused and shaded her eyes. "Look at all the new homes that are springing up all around! There's that neat little cottage over there in that dell, and the sturdy little farm just around the corner . . ."

"Yes . . ." Beth wasn't thinking about the town. Then she shrugged and said dispassionately, "This town is taking on a permanent look!"

"Now, if only things will simmer down. Let's forget our silly fears and trust God to take care of us," Dorie said brightly. "Forget about the rumors and enjoy yourself!"

The afternoon felt thin and cool and the horizon gave way to a windless landscape. They walked silently down the path, their footsteps rounding a dip in the road as they crossed the ravine. Dorie was right. Maybe the turmoil of the past few days was over. She would simply trust the Lord to care for the days that loomed ahead. What else was there?

Chapter 4

Sunday morning services at the Plymouth Congregational Church were over, and the congregation milled around outside, talking and visiting as usual.

Dorie and Beth moved to join Pastor Cordley. He had served the people who worshiped in the small stone building on the corner of Louisiana and Pinkney Streets since 1857, and they knew he appreciated their work with the children. Pastor Cordley's silver-gray hair and neatly trimmed beard looked distinguished and calm, though Andy maintained he looked "holy" when he stood behind the pulpit.

He was in deep conversation with a couple and their two young sons, apparent newcomers in town.

"Yes," he was saying in his resonant voice, "we do lack Sunday school materials for the children, but unfortunately that's just one of our many needs."

Beth hustled up beside him and the people he was addressing. "Pastor," she cut in, "Dorie and I overheard what you said.

We don't want to interrupt, but what of using the money we took in at the box social the other week? We'd hoped to use it to fix the drafty corners of the hall, but we really need to feed the children spiritually. We can always fix the rest of the church before winter sets in."

"Of course!" Reverend Cordley gave a vigorous nod. "That's a splendid idea. You are two of our best Sunday school teachers and know what the lack is." He paused and turned to the visitors. "The Howells have moved here recently from Massachusetts, and their two fine lads are Donnie and Karl. The family has chosen to worship with us and we welcome them heartily."

Hastily Beth thought of the kettle of chicken soup she had fixed for lunch. Should she invite them for dinner? By adding a cup or two of water and a handful of garden vegetables it could stretch enough to feed them all.

"Why not join us for lunch?" Beth burst out quickly. "If you don't mind a simple lunch of soup and fresh bread, you're welcome to come to our house."

The woman's face beamed. Beth noticed the merry brown eyes and the neat embroidered collar of the figured delaine dress. "How nice of you, Miss —"

"I'm Beth Davis. We'll be glad to have you join us. My father's around here somewhere and he'll bring you to our house up the street. I'm sure Andy will be delighted with the company of your two boys. They've probably already met in Sunday school."

"Then it's all arranged. We'll discuss the church school materials later, Beth." Pastor Cordley nodded briefly.

Beth took Dorie's arm as the two girls started to walk away. She turned to the Howells with a light wave of her hand. "We'll see you later. Pastor Cordley will introduce you to my father, I'm sure."

"It didn't take you long to get acquainted," Dorie laughed. "I hope your soup's adequate. If I can help with the meal —"

"No, I'll manage."

The two girls left the churchyard and hurried down the boardwalk. Suddenly Dan Wilcox appeared and barred Beth's way. "Hey, not so fast, m'love. I haven't seen or heard from you in a week. I thought you'd be ready to tell me what you've been up to. How about me sticking my feet under your table at dinner? That would give us a good chance to talk."

Beth's glance leaped wildly in dismay, and she frowned. "The — the Howells are fresh from Massachusetts and I've invited them to eat with us. I'm afraid there won't be room for any more at the table. Sorry, Dan."

Dan frowned and stalked away without a word.

Dorie laid a gentle hand on Beth's shoulder. "The man's jealous, Beth, or I miss my guess!"

Beth was in no mood to discuss Dan's feelings for her. At least he'd been in church for a change. Probably only because there had been no new calf to nurse this morning. Why did Dan Wilcox calling her "m'love" bother her so? Was it that he assumed there was something between them? She sniffed. What was more important at the moment was to put a hearty company meal on the table. She was glad she'd baked an apple pie yesterday.

Beth hugged her friend. "I have to get home to put the final touches on the meal, like adding a bit of water to the soup pot and setting the table. I'll see you soon, Dorie!"

After changing into a simple gingham frock and a blue-checked apron when she got home, she made her way to the kitchen. She stoked the fire in the range and took a clean white tablecloth from the sideboard. Then she set the table with the blue Spode china and got out the soup tureen. She took a loaf of fresh wheat bread from the cupboard and set bowls of peach preserves and fresh butter on the table. With a serrated knife she cut the apple pie. Already the hearty aroma of chicken soup swimming with vegetables and spices wafted through the house.

She heard a babble of voices coming up the path and hurried to the door, wiping her hands on her apron.

"I know my daughter will have a meal fit for a king to fill your stomachs," Pa was saying jovially as Beth opened the kitchen door. "It's good to have a houseful of guests, especially from our home state of Massachusetts! And you two fine boys will be company for Andy. We are truly blessed." He ushered them into the kitchen while Beth quickly filled the coffeepot with water and added fresh-ground coffee.

"If Mama were only with us," she said after greeting the guests. "She died when Andy was only five. Here, sit down while I finish the preparations, Mrs. Howell," she added, pointing to the sturdy kitchen chairs.

Mrs. Howell brushed her words aside. "Let me help. Shall I put the napkins beside the plates? And my name's Amy! My, the soup smells delicious! You're so young to be cooking for a family, Beth."

"Oh, I've cooked since I was ten. And I've learned to kill a chicken and fix a meal since Mama — left us." She glanced at the neatly spread table. It looked presentable. "Now I think we're ready to eat."

As the guests seated themselves at the table, Andy between the two boys, Pa bowed his head.

"Thank you, Father, for these guests who have joined us for this meal. We are thankful that they will be a part of our congregation and become our friends. Grant that we'll all help Lawrence to grow into a strong corner for the gospel and for free-state Kansas. . . ."

After Beth had dipped out generous helpings of hearty soup into the bowls, the three boys dove into their meal. They laughed and chattered as they spread slices of bread with jam.

"Wow! Good ol' peach jam!" Donnie praised.

"Let's get together to play ball," Karl suggested between mouthfuls.

"But not on Sunday!" Andy burst out.

"Why not? What's wrong with playing ball on Sunday?"

"Uh — Pastor Cordley says it don't please God to do worldly stuff on the Lord's day. He also says a tree planted on Sunday won't grow."

"Never heard of such a thing," Donnie snorted.

"Well, how about tomorrow then?"

Beth smiled as she got up to pour coffee. "I'm sure that will be fine. Andy has had trouble keeping out of mischief. It's good that you boys know how to play ball. It'll keep you occupied."

As she sat down at the table again, she served pie to the boys and sent them outside after they had eaten.

"Tell us something about Lawrence's churches. We noticed there are at least five or six. This indicates a strong spiritual tone in town," Amy Howell said.

"Yes, that's true. Besides ours there are Presbyterian, Baptist, Episcopal, Catholic and Methodist and some others. But the border raids are affecting the community because of the trauma Kansas has been through in the past," Beth said. "God knows how we must rely on Him."

"How is that?" Earl asked, picking up his fork and cutting a bite-size piece of pie.

Pa set down his coffee cup. "We free-staters built our churches as monuments to faith and freedom, but there are some proslavery folks who're still angry because Kansas became a free state instead of slave. Many community decisions are made under the church roof, and we must constantly decide how to carry on and how to work until slavery is uprooted and destroyed!"

"But if the free-state faction won, how can it still be a problem? Shouldn't the opposition accept this mandate of the people?" Earl countered.

"It should, but some of the Southerners are still tryin' to cause trouble because of this very thing," Pa said. "Since Lawrence has such a strong free population some still want to punish the town for this."

"Especially people like border ruffians. There's William Quantrill, as he calls himself now," Beth added hesitantly. "He visits Lawrence every now and then, though I can't quite believe he's as bent on causing mischief as many do." She got up from the table for the coffeepot again. "He seemed — at one time — like such a quiet, personable young man."

"Not after the way he humiliated you — and your fine supper — at the box social the other week!" Pa snorted. "Besides, he's been in one fracas after another. I heard in church this mornin' that he's been lurkin' on the north side of the river again. Some folks seem to think he won't dare to try anything, but I'm not so sure." Pa sighed heavily.

"Isn't he the one who was arrested at that proslavery town Paola but the judge couldn't find reason to hold him and let him go?" Earl said.

Pa sniffed. "Oh, he's never far from trouble, some say. Others don't believe he'll be a problem. It's hard to say one way or another."

"That judge was probably biased! We like this town and want to see it thrive," Earl Howell said. "The streets are wide and there's an air of permanence about it. Eldridge House is an excellent hotel. And they tell me Lawrence has about 2,000 population."

"Yes, and more folks comin' in almost daily."

The meal ended and, after the Howells left, Pa went out to check on the stock while Beth cleared away the dishes. She was perplexed. She wasn't sure of herself anymore. The man who called himself William Quantrill was certainly an enigma.

Before she had finished the dishes, Beth heard the pounding of horses' hooves and looked up to see Dan's familiar figure ride into the yard. Was he still looking for a bite of lunch? Or female attention? She shook her head. What an obstinate man!

He doffed his gray felt hat as she invited him in. "Would you like a piece of pie?" she asked politely. "There's one piece left."

"Your company gone?" Dan slid into a chair and nodded expectantly. "Pie sounds fine."

Beth got out a clean saucer and deftly served the piece of pie, juices dripping around the edges. "How about coffee?"

"Sounds fine too, if it's still hot."

Pouring a cupful from the gray-enameled pot on the stove, she set it before him. "It's still warm. The Howells will be a fine addition to the community, not to mention the church, don't you think?"

"Did you tell them about the guerrillas that're bothering us?"

"Guerrillas? Oh, they haven't really done much harm so far, so why does everyone assume they're causing problems?" she said testily.

"Don't you? Beth, do you believe that border ruffian Quantrill is hangin' around town just for fun?"

She sat down and clasped her hands in front of her. "Quantrill? But how do we know what he's up to?"

Dan gulped down his coffee and pushed his empty cup aside. "That's just it, Beth-dear. It's getting bad enough! Some men in town have just about decided to join the state militia and chase him and his cohorts out of Jackson County. Maybe it's not a bad idea. At least we'd be rid of him here. Don't you agree?"

"What do *you* think, Dan Wilcox? About the state militia getting him away from here?"

He shrugged his broad shoulders. "I'm thinking about joining the militia."

"What of your farm? You're getting all set to prove your claim. What would that do to your plans?" Beth's voice was level.

He got up, pushed his chair aside and started toward the door. Then he stopped and gazed anxiously at her, his dark-blue eyes gentle.

"Beth, I love you — you know that, don't you? If I knew William Clark Quantrill was out to destroy our town, I'd feel compelled to help chase him as far as I could. For your sake . . ."

Then he burst out of the house, his words ringing in her ears. *He loves me?* She shook her head. She felt nothing for this handsome farmer, of course. Why should it bother her if he went on such a ridiculous mission? After all, what they knew about Quantrill was gossip. Or was it? She couldn't be sure anymore.

Chapter 5

On Monday morning Beth lugged pails of water into the large iron kettle and built a fire under it for the weekly washing. The sky was a brilliant, blazing blue, and sunlight hammered on the round knolls that stretched to Mount Oread.

The fresh, clean aroma of lye soap drifted from Beth's washtubs as she lathered Pa's workpants and Andy's denim trousers. She strung the clean clothes on the line beside the house, then paused as she watched Andy and the two Howell boys racing around the backyard, yelling "bang-bang," pretending to shoot at each other.

"You're a bushwhacker!" Andy yelled at Karl, and Donnie rushed toward him shouting. "And you're a jayhawker!" Karl shot back.

What were the boys doing playing "bushwhacker and jayhawker"? Everyone in town knew that the border ruffians (called bushwhackers) favored slavery while the jayhawkers were those who followed James Lane's free-soil Unionists. Were the boys acting out what was going on according to community rumors? There were so many rumors floating through town. Not long before, the troops of Missouri State Guards had ridden into Humboldt and burned homes and stores. Apparently the Union militia had threatened to kill Quantrill, so he had gone into hiding. Posses patrolled the countryside to prevent another raid. As a result of all the fighting, Quantrill had organized a band of border ruffians which became known as "Quantrill's Band." It was said the band wore shirts with V-shaped fronts and tails with four huge pockets. Also they seemed better equipped: they had more guns than the free-staters and used .44 caliber Colt navy revolvers, while some carried shotguns, muskets or Sharp's rifles. Because of Mayor Collamore's instructions, Lawrence citizens were meagerly armed.

When bushwacker Dick Yeager rode into Council Grove, a nearby town, one day, no one was prepared to confront him. As citizens haphazardly hid in the town, Yeager rode to the dentist's office and asked to have a tooth pulled.

"I'll pull your tooth if you'll spare the town," the quavering dentist had told him frantically. Shortly after, the man left.

This talk was all over town. Beth sighed

and shook her head. She knew of the wild backgrounds of the guerrillas, and by now she didn't believe that this man who called himself William Clark Quantrill was a leader young boys should emulate.

"Boys!" she shouted fiercely, looking up from the dripping trousers she was hanging on the line. "Please find something else to play! Pretend you're crossing the Kansas River — or something less terrifying! But no more vicious war games!"

Slowly their shrill yelling and bang-banging stopped, and reluctantly they wandered down to the ravine. She cleaned up the washing equipment and went into the house.

When Pa came home from the mill he drew off his hat wearily and sank down into a chair, waiting for his evening meal.

"Things are in a real state in town," he said, wiping his brow with a red handkerchief. "Mayor Collamore has received a letter from Colonel Ewing's staff that's a real concern for our town. Council Grove and Emporia have received threats about being attacked. Scouts report that forces of bushwhackers are gatherin' to attack 'a Kansas town'!"

Beth finished folding the freshly washed pants and shirts. Then she began supper

60

preparations. "Wonder which Kansas town they're talking about," she said with a catch in her voice. She broke eggs into the skillet and tried to stifle a chill that ran down her back.

"When you think of it, the town could well be Lawrence," Pa mused, picking up *The Kansas Tribune*. "Colonel Ewing's command is most inadequate. What's more — Lawrence is one of the most well-heeled communities. And since Quantrill's fiercest enemy is James Lane and the town has many folks strong for the Union cause —"

"Like John Speer, editor of *The Tribune*," Beth said quietly, "Captain Banks, Provost Marshal of Kansas; Judge Louis Carpenter; Judge Sam Riggs; Reverend Fisher, chaplain of Lane's force. Oh, Pa, what are we to do?"

Pa drew a deep sigh. "Lawrence will be picketed and patrolled, I'm sure. They're even plannin' to roll the cannon up on Mount Oread. I hope that'll scare off anyone with ideas to attack the town."

Beth sighed again as she stirred the scrambled eggs with a slotted spoon. She looked up from the stove, a deep frown touching her face.

"But how much of all this is rumor and how much is truth?" she demanded. "Everyone talking about all of this reminds me exactly of a flock of blackbirds squawking in the ravine. All talk and no substance!"

Pa laid down *The Tribune* and scratched his head. "That's one thing we don't know, Beth. If the reports of the scouts can't be proved . . ." he shook his head. She didn't know what to believe anymore either. It was true: some jayhawkers had tried to run down the Missourians who had earlier attacked Kansas, intent on "punishing" them.

"The only thing we can do is pray," she said finally as she stepped out the door and called Andy in for supper. The Howell boys had left and she had sent Andy to gather eggs.

"Did you boys have a good ballgame?" she asked Andy when he came in to wash up.

"I guess it was all right, but it was more funner to play bushwhackers and jayhawkers," he confessed with a sly gleam in his eyes.

"Don't forget what I told you," Beth snapped. "We have enough to worry about with all the rumors. Let's not talk about that anymore!"

After supper Pa left the house, taking Andy with him. "We want to see how the Eldridge House is coming along. It's said to be the finest hotel in the state," he added as they left.

After she had cleared the dishes away, Beth stepped outside into the fresh evening air. The day had been hot and humid, and a watercolor sunset brightened the soft twilight sky with vivid streaks of orange and pink. The sun still teetered over the horizon, a round muted light coming through thinning layers of clouds. But a brooding danger as gray and dark as winter seemed to hang over the town. Beth hurried inside and lit the lamp. She got out Andy's trousers and had just threaded her needle when Dan rode up and knocked on the door. Laying aside her sewing, she asked him in.

"Your father here?" he asked, seeming agitated.

"He and Andy went out to see what's going on at the Eldridge House. I hear it's just about completed."

"Quite an elegant affair, I hear. A group of men are planning to meet there soon to arrange for a new railroad coming into town," he said. "Also the bridge across the river will soon be finished. The town's really growing."

"Yes, it is. Now if people would only put aside those ridiculous rumors and just let it grow!" she said, turning up the wick of the lamp. The brooding darkness seemed to fill the room, making it seem more somber than ever, and she stifled a shiver. "Did you want to see Pa about something important?"

"I wondered if he'd heard more about the border ruffians. Desperadoes Cole Younger and Frank Yeager are reported to be a part of Quantrill's band. If that ruffian hasn't learned yet how to be ruthless, these two will teach him!"

Angrily she whirled on him. "You're so naive! You believe anything! If it is true, our town can take care of itself! How about Captain Lane? He and his men get rowdy too, yet most people don't consider them dangerous!"

Dan got up and paced across the room. "Beth, you still aren't fully convinced that Quantrill is bad news!" he spat out. "When Captain Pike and the Ninth Kansas Volunteers were stationed at Aubry they noticed a large force of soldiers passing by — a large force!"

"And what did Captain Pike do about it?" she asked.

"Nothing."

"Nothing! Didn't they find out whose forces they were?"

"Well —"

"I doubt that they even notified other Union attachments in the area. What kind of men does he have in his command, anyhow? If Quantrill is considered so dangerous, why doesn't anyone *do* something?" Beth was very angry now. It seemed so senseless to practically ignore the dangers around them — if they were real — and just *talk* about them!

"I don't know, Beth!" he shrugged his broad shoulders. "They just don't believe all this spells trouble, I guess. They still don't think Quantrill will do anything stupid."

"Can you see why I have had my doubts about all those rumors, when no one seems to take them seriously?"

"Oh, they've sent out scouts, I hear. Still —"

"Still, everyone is so weak-kneed they're afraid to make a move. And what about the militia you were so sure could do something?" she demanded.

Dan gave Beth a long, level look, stalked out of the house, got on his horse and rode away.

Chapter 6

After Dan left, silence seemed to echo throughout the house. *Have I been too harsh with Dan?* she asked herself. *He's been so sure that Quantrill meant it when he threatened the town.* And what had Quantrill implied when he had told her at the box social that she hadn't heard the last of him?

Lord, she prayed when she went to bed that night, *please take care of us all. We must depend on Your leading.*

No more threats came from the border ruffians the next week or two, even though the military protection Mayor Collamore had asked from Brigadier General Ewing consisted of a mere handful of men the mayor had ordered to the north side of the river.

The next afternoon Beth met Dan at the Guild Grocery Store where she had gone for flour and sugar.

"No one has heard any more threats for the past week," she scoffed as she waited for the clerk to figure up her bill. "Maybe the rumormongers will have to eat their words one of these days. Besides, work has resumed on the bridge across the Kansas River. It'll afford more protection — if that's what we need."

"Yes, it was halted for a while," Dan said, leaning against a pickle barrel. "It's high time the bridge is finished. With all the immigrants coming from Independence on the Missouri side, it will improve transportation."

A ferry had been established in 1855 by two men who had come to Lawrence as settlers. The ferry was no more than a flatbed propelled by ropes stretched across the river and aided by the current.

At first a bridge was not considered feasible because of quicksand and unstable banks, but a visit from a competent engineer in 1859 resulted in the Lawrence Bridge Company charter, and a bridge had begun to span the surging river. Work was progressing well although it was still months from being completed.

Beth relaxed when the rumors grew fewer, and people seemed to forget their fears. It seemed they had bobbed up and down with uncertainty for weeks; now everything was quiet. Everyone seemed agog with the completion of the Eldridge House.

One afternoon she and Dorie walked to the hotel to see for themselves how this splendid structure had progressed. The frescoes around the eaves were ornate, the trimming elaborate and the chandeliers magnificent. Colonel Eldridge had brought his family from the East to take charge of what had once been the Free State Hotel. The Free State had been torched by John Brown and his men seven years before. The Eldridge House was built on the very same foundation. Colonel Eldridge had once been a delegate to the first Republican convention in Philadelphia which had been active to admit Kansas into the Union as a free state. The hotel was finally completed and served as headquarters for free-state conventions.

As the two girls crossed Massachusetts Street and walked into the lobby and down the lush, carpeted corridors they stopped now and then to admire the gleaming mirrors, the elaborately carved woodwork.

"My, this is about as fancy a place as I've ever seen," Dorie breathed. "Who would've ever suspected Kansas — or Lawrence — would build such a fine place!"

Beth laughed. "I guess we should have visited before. Perhaps we wouldn't have been so stunned by its grandeur."

"I'm glad you came with me, Beth. For so long I've wanted to see it," Dorie beamed.

"Frankly, I should've been home working in the garden this afternoon but I turned the job over to Andy — for once. I've wanted to see the Eldridge since it's been finished."

"I hope it will never be burned again!" Dorie added fervently.

"Let's hope no part of this town will ever see a devastating fire," Beth said soberly. "It certainly is a very lovely place."

"I wonder," Dorie said after a thoughtful pause, "if the Underground Railroad in Topeka still transports slaves that come through here? George French seems to think so."

"I wouldn't be surprised. After all, so many slaves reached actual freedom after they were declared free!"

The afternoon passed swiftly, and the two girls strolled home.

That night when Pa came in, Beth's beef stew already bubbled on the stove. Andy had chopped wood for the cookstove and brought in a panful of carrots from the garden after she had given stern orders to help her instead of romping around town with the Howell boys.

"Somethin' sure smells good," he sniffed when he came in. "Beth, no matter what happens, I hope you'll always be here to fix good food!"

"When she gets married, she won't be around to do much cookin', son," Pa said, coming into the door.

"Married!" she scoffed. "Who is there who'd want to get tied to someone like me?"

"Dan Wilcox shows up around here aplenty," Andy said, scooting to the table. "He don't come here just to look at the wallpaper."

Pa laughed. "Well, if he's lookin' for a good girl, he's come to the right place." He paused. "You haven't encouraged him much, it seems to me, Beth. Provin' up his claim takes a lot of time, I s'pose. But don't brush off such a handsome young man too long!"

Beth moistened her dry lips and frowned as she carried the stew to the table. "Pa — I'm not so sure Dan is a Christian. Oh, yes — he comes to church when it suits him but as for salvation . . ."

"Yes, of course. You must be careful. God's Word says not to be unequally yoked."

"That's just it. He — he's let me know he cares about me, but — well, I won't marry a man who doesn't feel the same about the Lord as I do."

"Just don't brush him aside completely. But how about Lynn Nelson? He does a fine job helpin' Pastor Cordley with Bible studies and such."

She set the pot on the table. "Pa — are you trying to get rid of me?"

He laughed uproariously. "Not at all! I just want to give you a nudge — not to avoid a Christian man."

"Well, right now I'm satisfied with where I am. Pastor Cordley is depending on Dorie and me to help build up the Sunday school and we're helping him and Lynn."

"Yeah, he sure keeps us hoppin' with memorizin' Scriptures. Now it's Isaiah we're battlin' with," Andy grunted.

"God's Word is worthy to be memorized. One never knows when we will need it most."

Beth cut fresh, spicy gingerbread into neat squares and they finished their meal in silence.

"Dorie and I went out to see the Eldridge House this afternoon," Beth said after a long pause. "I didn't realize it was so fancy. No wonder it's been called the finest hotel in Kansas."

"Yes, Jim Yates and I went to the Eldridge for coffee this afternoon. It's certainly a fine place."

"Pa! Since when do you go out for coffee during a busy, dusty day at the mill?" Beth asked, as she started to clear the table.

"Actually, Jim and I went on an errand in that part of town. When we talked to Colonel Eldridge about some supplies, he invited us in for rolls and coffee."

"But you were all dusty, Pa! Didn't you feel out of place?" Beth grimaced. "To enter a nice place in your work clothes —"

"Well, actually — no. When we came in, a man named Taylor happened to meet us at the door and seemed congenial and asked a lot of questions about the mill."

"I bet he wanted to ask about wood to build another shop. Or a home," Andy said, jumping from the table and heading for the door. "That's what most strangers do when they come to town."

"He did remark about our nice wide streets and fine stores. But —"

"What, Pa? What else did he say?" Beth prodded.

Pa shook his head. "He wanted to know — about the rumors floatin' all over town, and what I thought would happen. Still —"

"I hope you told him there haven't been any more rumors for over a week. That people in Lawrence are smart enough not to be taken in by a lot of talk!" she snapped.

"Well — no, I didn't say much about that. He — he seemed too curious, in my opinion. A complete stranger askin' —"

"Maybe he's just scouting out what Lawrence is like, if he wants to move here."

Pa shook his head. "No. Somethin' about him disturbed me. I don't know exactly why."

"Oh, Pa! You're too suspicious. Just because someone comes to town and asks a few questions . . ."

"Not a few, Beth. All about the mill and all about the Eldridge. Even the armory." He shook his head. "I don't like it — don't like it a bit!"

He pushed his chair aside from the table and went to the door. "I'll check the stock and make sure the mill's locked up."

After he had gone, Beth shrugged her shoulders. *Where's Pa's faith?* she thought. *If all the rumors we've heard these past weeks were to come to pass, Lawrence would've been attacked weeks ago!*

Chapter 7

Beth checked the calendar after she cleared away the evening meal. It was Thursday, August 20, 1863 — and vague uneasiness seeped through her. She didn't understand why. After all, the rumors of an impending attack had died; apparently no more threats had been received.

I'm not really afraid, she reminded herself firmly. Most citizens in town refused to believe Quantrill's threats of attack. Yet his words to her at the box social about not having seen the last of him nagged at her, and she shivered a little. If she gave in to her fears it was a sign that she was beginning to believe the "rumormongers."

She shrugged her shoulders and went outside to call Andy in for bed. Pa had gone to lock up the mill and would soon be back.

The sun was already setting and daylight was waning with a few reluctant stars winking in a murky sky. A faint afterglow hung over the hills in the west like the spilled rays of a rainbow.

"Andy?" she called sharply. "Where are you?"

She heard the sound of running footsteps as he bounded barefoot around the corner of the house.

"Beth? What did ya want?"

"It's almost bedtime. I wondered if you had shut the henhouse door and penned up the dogs."

"Oh, I closed the coops all right. I know that's my job. But why do such a stupid thing like shutting up the dogs? We never do — except in winter."

"Well," Beth paused in the doorway of the kitchen, "I'd feel safer that way. I was a bit uneasy."

He sauntered toward the kitchen and stuck his head in the doorway. "Because of the bushwhackers? And you're the one who said that the rumors are just so much talk. Why would you get scared tonight? I thought the scare-talks had quit."

She motioned him inside. "Those border ruffians bragged about planning to attack 'a Kansas town,' and I didn't —"

"How do we know the Kansas town they're talkin' about is Lawrence? It could be Emporia or Council Grove. They've hassled them both before."

"You could be right." She nodded and got

out an old gray enameled washbasin. "Better wash your face and get ready for bed. Pa's gone to check on the mill, and he'll be back shortly. He doesn't like for us to be up late, you know. Now, after you've washed, I'll hear those verses Pastor Cordley wants you to memorize."

With a sigh Andy splashed his face noisily in the water for a few minutes, then reached for the old towel and rubbed it briskly.

"Now wash your feet."

"I sure worked over those verses, Beth," he muttered, "but they don't come easy." He dabbled his toes in the basin.

She picked up the Bible from the clock shelf and paged through it until she found Isaiah 43. "I'm glad you've been working on them. Let's hear you say them."

Andy squatted on the bare floor and leaned back on his elbows. His freckled face looked rather bored.

"Well, here I go. 'Fear not: for I have redeemed thee, I have called thee by thy name —' Do you mean God actually called Andy Davis? How come I didn't hear Him?"

"Go on! Don't dawdle!"

" 'Thou art mine.' Yeah, I guess that's true enough."

"What's the next verse?"

"Uh — 'When thou passest through the

waters, I will be with thee; and through the rivers, they shall not overflow thee: when thou walkest through the fire, thou shalt not be burned; neither shall the flame kindle upon thee. For I am the LORD thy God, the Holy One of Israel, thy Saviour.' Sounds scary, if you ask me!"

Beth patted his shoulder. "You did a fine job. I hope the Howell boys know them as well as you. It means that God has promised to be with us. Now say your prayers and scoot to bed!" She carried a lighted lamp into the room he and Pa shared as Andy pattered after her.

After he rattled through his prayers and bounced into his bed, she placed a kiss on his damp forehead and started for the door.

"Beth, do ya hafta kiss me like that? I'm nine years old!"

"That's all right. I'd kiss you even if you were ninety!" She turned down the lamp wick with a grin and started for the door. "Good night, Andy. Sleep well."

She heard a halfhearted mumble from his pillow and partly closed the door to the bedroom. Washing her own face, she unplaited her braids and combed out her long hair that spilled like a shower of silk down her back. Then she went into her bedroom and slipped into her light summer nightgown.

Just then she heard Pa come into the kitchen. She drew on her blue percale robe and hurried into the other room.

"Beth? You're not in bed?"

She blinked in the dim lamplight. "No. I first heard Andy's verses and his prayers. Did you see anything suspicious out there? It seems like a — a spooky night."

He sat down in his walnut rocker and smiled. "Nothing suspicious. There's a big meeting at the Eldridge House these days for men interested in building the Kansas Pacific Railroad, you know, and I assume strangers have booked rooms there. Are you still worried?"

She shook her head slowly. "Not — not really. It's just that — somehow I've had this eerie feeling and I don't understand it!"

"Well, let's just trust the Lord to watch over us. That's all we can do."

"Andy's verses are full of 'fear nots,' so I guess that's the answer. Good night, Pa."

She went back into her bedroom to open the window and look out. The yellow prairie moon hung from the sky and she listened for strange noises. All she heard was the soft murmur of doves in the barn and the tick-tacking of insects in the brush. Everything seemed quiet and peaceful. Maybe she was just being silly.

Kneeling down, she began to pray — for God's protection, for Pastor Cordley and the church, for Lynn Nelson's work with the young people, Dorie and for the patrol north of town. *And Lord, I pray for Dan Wilcox to know You as his Savior!*

She crawled into bed and closed her eyes. Soon her eyelids drooped. Before long she was sound asleep.

It seemed she had slept for hours when something stirred through her subconsciousness. Suddenly she heard a popping sound.

Groping for the edge of her sheet, she sat up and blinked. Who'd pop firecrackers in August so early in the morning?

A pink sky met her eyes as she looked out the window. Sunrise? The staccato sound of shooting echoed through the dawn. Then she smelled smoke. Fumbling, she pushed aside the scrim curtains to get a full view and saw flames shooting up into the sky to the north. Then realization hit her. Guerrillas? "Oh no . . ." she gasped. The whole town seemed on fire!

Chapter 8

Shivering with horror, Beth grabbed a shawl, pulled it over her nightgown and peeked through the window again. Just then another blast of gunfire erupted somewhere to the east, and she jerked the curtain back quickly. Was it really true? Had Quantrill made good his threat to burn the town? *You haven't seen the last of me* echoed through her mind and she grew limp with fear.

Praying, she stumbled through the house. Pa staggered from the bedroom, his clothes thrown on haphazardly, his gray hair awry. He stood at the kitchen door, his hand on the doorknob. Did he plan to go outside?

"Pa!" she screamed, her voice ragged with fear.

"I'll be back when I find out what's happening," he said as he slipped quietly out of the house. Where was Pa going? When would the raiders ride to their street and burn down their house? In the dim background she heard the shrill neighing of horses, gunshots and more screams, and as she glanced wildly through the window she heard another burst of gunfire and a cry of horrendous alarm. Andy! He must be frightened, and she hurried to his cot. He was kneeling by the window, his face frozen in fear. *Oh, dear God, please take care of my brother, my father . . .* She knelt beside Andy and placed a shaking arm around his shoulders. He winced at her touch, and she whispered into his ear.

"Andy — it's me! I — please — stay here, and don't go outside!"

He turned his stricken face to her, fighting childish tears. "Beth, it's awful, ain't it? Where's Pa?"

With a corner of her robe she dabbed at her own tears and shook her head stonily. "He — went outdoors to see what's happening."

"But —"

"I'm frightened, Andy, and I need extra comfort too." She got up from Andy's side and went to her room, took off her robe and slipped into a gray dress. Aimlessly she tied her hair back into a loose knot with a ribbon. Then she picked up her Bible and returned to Andy as she paged through it.

Pausing at Isaiah 43, she began to read aloud, verses 2 and 3: "When thou passest through the waters, I will be with thee; and through the rivers, they shall not overflow

thee: when thou *walkest through the fire*. . . ."
She paused and choked back a sob, then continued to read, "through the fire, thou shalt not be burned; *neither shall the flame kindle upon thee*. For I am the LORD thy God, the Holy One of Israel, thy Saviour."

Then her gaze dropped to verse 5: "Fear not: for I am with thee."

"Oh, dear God . . . God . . . God . . ." she wept. "Please protect us! Please don't leave us. . . ." Her prayer was an agony of pleading.

As a dull feeling of peace fell over her she walked slowly, numbly, into the kitchen to prepare breakfast. The clock said it was a little after 6 o'clock. She wanted to run, but she knew it wasn't safe, at least not until Pa came back. She wasn't hungry — no one would want to eat either, she was sure, but they'd need sustenance. Mechanically she set out a pitcher of milk and thick, crusty wedges of bread. The words from Isaiah strengthened her; the Lord would take care of them.

Andy had changed into shirt and trousers and wandered woodenly to the kitchen table. "I'm not really hungry, Beth. But I want a drink of milk."

She took a tumbler from the cupboard and filled it to the brim. "I know how you feel, Andy. But as you say, you need something in your stomach. How about a slice of butter bread too?"

He hesitated, then nodded perceptibly. "Well — all right," and pulled out a chair and sat down. "I wish Pa was here," he added anxiously.

"I know. So do I. But I think he wanted to scout around to see what's happening. Let's pray he'll be back soon."

She poured a glass of milk for herself and sat down across the yellow oilcloth-covered table from him and took a few sips.

"If we only knew what's going on," she whispered. "Few of us believed Quantrill would actually do as he threatened. But —" she sighed and toyed with her half-empty glass.

"The noises and all seem to be to the northeast part of town, don't you think?" Andy ventured after finishing his bread. "They most likely came into town across the river. If they did, they had to get through Captain Lane's camp. I hope that's a part of the reason for the shootin' and the militia's gunnin' 'em down. That Quantrill's a rotten man!"

Beth shrugged and shook her head solemnly. "Andy, God's in control. We've got to believe that! Remember the verses you learned?"

"But with all that shootin' it don't sound very promisin'!"

Beth was silent. He was so right. Then the door burst open and Pa barreled inside, looking harried and haggard.

"I sneaked down the street a ways and met a few folks. It seems the ruffians're attackin' the east part of town mostly; along the ravine we should be fairly safe yet," he said. "But people in the rest of town — it seems from what I've heard that there is a list of the ones who are to be killed. Mostly prominent townsfolk and businessmen."

"Do you know who they are?"

Pa stroked his chin thoughtfully. "Captain Lane was number one on Quantrill's list. Quantrill's made no secret of hatin' him for being head of the free-state movement. Also Rev. Hugh Fisher who has served as Lane's army chaplain, Editor Speer and many others. Anyone who stood in the proslavery way."

"Well, that should leave us out," Andy said with a stab at cheerfulness, "includin' you, Pa. Remember, you gave Quantrill money once to buy a meal, didn't ya?"

Pa's face looked grim. "But I'm a businessman! I work in the mill!" Pa countered. "Fortunately Quantrill's given orders to leave women and children alone."

"But what about me?" Beth said. "Remember what he said to me at the box social when I turned down his bid to share the meal I fixed?" Her voice was weak.

"That's true," Pa nodded. "We've no arms —"

"I still have my bean shooter!" Andy chortled. "I'll help perteck ya."

"You stay in the house, Andy," Pa ordered sternly, getting to his feet and heading for the door. "Let's leave the fightin' to the militia."

"Please stay here, Pa!" Beth cried, startled at his move toward the door. "Let the militia do what they're called to do!"

"But I must know what's goin' on. Is the militia doin' anything?"

"Oh, Pa —"

He paused, and his jaw slacked. "I — I pray I'm wrong, but from the news I heard a few minutes ago, most of the militia had to take their arms to the armory days ago!" Then he stalked out the door.

Beth and Andy stared at each other. What would happen next? In the distance the sound of shooting and yelling increased and Beth shuddered.

"I — I prayed in my room for God to keep us safe," Andy said wistfully after a pause. "I also — asked Jesus into my heart, in case —" he stopped awkwardly.

"In case He didn't?" Beth asked gently. "Claiming Christ as one's Savior is something everyone should do — whether in danger or not. I'm so glad you did it, Andy. It makes me feel good!"

He nodded silently.

She looked up, startled, as a clatter of horses' hoofs sounded near the door, and she didn't miss the look of terror in Andy's eyes. *Had the guerrillas come to carry out Quantrill's threat?* Just then she heard Dan's voice as he slammed the kitchen door open.

"You all right?" he yelled. "I heard the noise clear out on my farm and I wanted to check to make sure you were safe."

"Y-yes," Beth faltered. "But Pa's gone out and I'm worried!"

"He'd better hide if he doesn't want to meet the rebels' wrath. Why don't you and Andy ride out to the farm with me where you'll be safe?"

"We can't leave!" Beth cried out. "We don't know where Pa is, and he'd be worried sick if we weren't here — in case he returns!"

"I see. Old man Allen who lives in that brick house beyond the hill owns four navy guns which he never turned in. When a bunch of guerrillas stopped at his place, they were going to shoot him. But when he told them about the guns and threatened to fire them, they skedaddled. He said reports were that Skaggs, a former Lawrence pro-slavery yokel, had torn down the flag at the military camp north of town and tied it to his horse's tail — after the band killed the soldiers."

Beth's face grew white. "The — soldiers killed? Oh, no . . ." Then she shakily poured a glass of milk for Dan. "Here's something to sustain you, Dan."

"Thanks, Beth. As for the militia —"

The shots sounded nearer, and through the window Beth could see flames and smoke curling up from a house perhaps a block away.

"I thought the militia was to protect Lawrence!" she cried.

"Remember — they weren't allowed to keep their arms. And then I heard about Rev. Michael Hummer. When they threatened him, he appealed to them in the name of Jesus Christ, and said he was formerly from the South but was against violence. He said his sympathies were for the South. He was ordered to stop interfering but when he refused, the guerrillas shot him. Luckily he wasn't killed."

"Oh, how ruthless they are!" Beth moaned, clapping her hands over her ears to shut out the noise of gunfire.

"I also heard what went on at the Eldridge House."

"Eldridge House? Surely they didn't —"

"Well, those guerrillas don't have a heart, you know. They rode down Massachusetts Street shootin' at everyone in sight. Just as they reached the hotel the gong sounded to waken the sleeping guests. The guerrillas thought it was a warning signal and yelled at them to come out. Captain Banks, Kansas Provost Marshal, who was one of the guests, came to the door waving a sheet. Quantrill asked if the guests would surrender. Yes, said Banks, if their lives would be spared, which Quantrill promised. Then he stormed inside the hotel and robbed the guests. Remember, some were wealthy officials who had spent the night there, planning for the new railroad. Then the guerrillas set the Eldridge House on fire."

At a sound by the door, Beth looked up. Pa slipped inside quietly and sat down at the table.

"Pa!" Beth gasped. "Please don't leave again. Where were you?"

"I kept out of sight of the raiders through the ravine where I hid. But there I got more news of others who were hidin' there. It seems the guerrillas had orders to kill every man and burn every house, which might include ours, if they reach us!"

Beth's face blanched.

"Well," Dan chuckled in a low voice, "some have escaped. Remember Mrs. Gossett, who has that fancy flower garden? When the raiders reached the house to burn it, she stalled them off by engaging them in talk. She met them bravely with, 'Good morning, men! You've come to see my flowers? Good!' Quantrill halted his men. 'What do you think of them?'

" 'They're fine,' he answered.

" 'Too pretty to be burned!' one of the men piped up.

"Then Quantrill whirled around. 'I'll shoot the first man who torches them! March on!'

"Meanwhile her husband sneaked out the back way," he added.

Pa and Dan chuckled at the story but Beth shook her head angrily. "How dare the two of you laugh at something so — so utterly inhuman?"

Dan sobered. "But Mr. Gossett got away. I'm sorry this upset you, Beth-dear," he said solemnly. "The way she outwitted them struck me as funny. I still think a spy tipped the raiders off."

Could the Mr. Taylor who'd talked to Pa

have been a spy for Quantrill? Beth shook her head. She saw nothing funny about the story. She would long remember this nightmare — if she lived through it. To think of the men they knew who had already been killed or wounded was almost too much, and she laid her head in her arms and sobbed uncontrollably.

Chapter 9

Beth glanced nervously at the clock. It was nearly 9 a.m. Pa and Dan had gone out again. The rattle of gunfire seemed to grow vaguely less. Or was it only because her ears had grown accustomed to the steady noise of shots and screams? She stood in the doorway, stretched on tiptoe to see if she could see anything. Here and there she saw spurts of flame and heard the staccato rattle of bullets. Then she saw a woman, riding wildly from the north, her black hair blowing in the wind, heading toward the house.

"Dorie!" she gasped.

Crying bitterly, Dorie pulled her horse to an abrupt stop and slid to the ground in one quick jerk.

"Dorie!" Beth cried again. "Your family . . . ?"

"F-father's dead, Beth!" Dorie sobbed hysterically, "and the bushwhackers tried to b-b-burn down our h-h-house!"

"How about your mother? And Ed?"

Dorie gulped down her sobs as she sank into the chair Beth shoved toward her.

"She — Mother wouldn't leave my fa-

91

ther's body. As for Ed —" A fresh gasp of sobs raked through her body, and the small, brown-clad figure in the sooty merino slumped against the back of the chair. "I don't know — where Ed is! Oh, Beth, it's all too horrible. I saw men shot and tossed into the burning flames of the house next door. What if Ed . . . ? Oh, Beth, I'm so frightened!" Horrendous sobs wrenched from Dorie's throat, and she shook violently.

"Oh, Dorie!" Beth threw her arms around her friend. "How can you stand it?"

"I —" Dorie choked back her sobs. "I'm just numb. It's as though I can't feel anything. . . . After the men k-killed my father, they set f-f-fire to the — the house! Mother and I were hiding in the hackberry bushes near the kitchen door until the awful raiders left. We — we drew buckets of water from the well and finally we got the fire out. But —"

Beth felt a shudder grip her shoulders at the atrocity against the town, against her best friend. She held Dorie in her arms. "Dorie — Dorie — but you've been spared. God heard my prayers for your safety. Is your mother still at the house?"

Dorie nodded. "But she just *sits* there and refuses to leave. That's — that's where she is now!"

"She's welcome to come here if she'll

leave. Oh, Dorie, please know that I care very deeply about your father. If I can do anything . . ." Where was Pa? And where was Dan?

Just then Andy rushed up, his large brown eyes wide. "Downtown looks awful!" he yelled as he barreled into the house.

"Andy! I didn't know you left the house. What ever possessed you to disobey me?" Beth demanded angrily.

Andy dropped his head to his chest. "But Pa and Dan and me — Pa said I could go with them, and I didn't stop — to tell you. I guess you were too — too scared to notice when we left . . ."

"Yes," Beth said with a slow nod. "I was just so stunned with — everything. But please stay here now, Andy. No more leaving the house!"

"Downtown nobody paid attention to me. The Eldridge is a-blazin' like — horrible! As for Pa and Dan —"

"Where are they?" Beth cut in harshly. "Are they still downtown? If Pa —"

"They went to the church. Pa wanted to make sure everythin' was all right."

"And was it?" Beth's words were wooden.

"As far as we could tell. Pastor Cordley was standin' in the doorway, lookin' sad and troubled. Then he and Pa began to carry in the men who was shot. That's all I know. Dan brought me back here then."

"But where's Dan now?"

"He's checkin' the outside 'cause he wanted to make sure everything was all right here."

The smell of smoke and fire hung over the streets. Beth drew a sigh of shaky relief as she took Dorie into the kitchen and poured a fresh drink of water. Well, they'd been spared, praise God. Apparently Quantrill decided not to harass her after all.

Meanwhile, news of what was happening in town was drifting in. It seemed people had been taken by surprise when the terrorists stormed into town, tore into the saloons and got uproariously drunk, becoming even more violent than ever. At the Johnsons', Andy said, one group of raiders had dragged out four men, lined them all up and shot them. Another group grabbed two men and threw them into the fire of a burning house. . . . Andy went on and on, his voice hoarse.

Among people who had befriended Quantrill when he was a young unknown was Lydia Stone, whose father owned the City Hotel. She had nursed him when he was ill. Now the guerrillas whirled on her and tore a valuable ring from her finger.

Some women were abused, but most were only insulted.

"What about the mayor?" Beth interrupted.

Andy had heard about that, too. When Mayor Collamore had woken to the yelling and shots, he knew the raiders were after him. Panting heavily, he stumbled after his wife, who rushed him to a building attached to the house, where she quietly lowered him and the hired man into a well out of reach. The family was robbed, the house burned and so much heavy smoke billowed into the well that the two men died later.

It seemed a group of guerrillas robbed the clothing store next to the Eldridge House and shot the two clerks. Determined to put the pro-Union newspaper out of business and shoot Editor John Speer, the terrorists killed at least one of Speer's sons but Speer miraculously escaped.

Mrs. Hugh Fisher, wife of Captain Lane's chaplain, whisked her husband into the cellar where he hid behind a pile of dirt. The guerrillas were sure he was somewhere on the premises and sct fire to thc house. One guerrilla stayed behind to see that the house burned and to shoot Mr. Fisher when he came out. He even offered to help Mrs. Fisher move out the furniture. She lugged whatever she could manage outdoors and whipped at the flames, trying to douse the fire. Softly she called her husband when the raiders were out of earshot, threw a carpet over him and dragged the carpet into the backyard in the brush. Once outside, Mrs. Fisher tossed more household goods over his hiding place. Four guerrillas waited for him to come out of the burning house but didn't suspect he was under the rug.

Smoke and flames belched from house to house. Another woman and her husband hid in a cellar with a dilapidated entrance surrounded by tall jimsonweed, rattling eerily in the breeze. Four other men who knew about the cellar also hid with them and thus escaped the bushwhackers.

Andy paused for breath. "This is the best one," he told Beth. A certain Mr. Wichell, he said, known by his heavy beard, ran into the home of one of the residents for safety. The women in the house quickly shaved off his beard, dressed him in a long dress as an old woman and placed him by a table with bottles of medicine. One of the women sat nearby and fanned him. When the ruffians stormed in, the women asked them to take what they wanted but to please be awfully quiet, as "Aunt Betsy" was very ill, and the doctor said nothing must disturb her. The bushwhacker took one good look at "Aunt Betsy" and left.

Across the Kansas River north of town, Half Moon, a Delaware Indian from the reservation, helped a man ashore after he jumped into the murky water to escape. Half Moon was shot.

Andy ceased his storytelling and looked anxiously at Beth.

Beth knelt on the floor in prayer. Dorie cradled her head in her arms beside her.

The morning had grown warm and humid. High, puffy clouds sat heavily overhead without movement, and the heat was limp and stifling. A pall of smoke hung over the town as the sharp, acrid odor of burning wood saturated the air.

The two Howell boys banged on the kitchen door, and Beth answered.

"Is your father safe?" Beth whispered.

Karl nodded. "He wasn't on the list to be killed, but he told us to come here." Soon the three boys huddled in a corner and shot marbles.

Traces of tears still streaked Dorie's face when Dan came in with the news that the guerrillas were leaving town.

"Praise God . . . praise God . . ." Beth's face grew calm.

"Do you think we should help nurse the

wounded that have been carried into the church? It's the least we could do," Dorie said weakly.

"That is, if Dan will see us safely downtown. I'm still unsure — "

"Of course," Dan offered. "But what shall we do with the boys? This part of town is safer than most."

"Knowing Pa, he's helping with the wounded," Beth said raggedly.

"The boys will be all right — if they stay inside," Dan said. "Come on, girls — let's head for the church. I'm sure Pastor Cordley can use our help. I'll escort you to the church, then I'll hurry back here with the boys."

Beth paused and looked at her young brother firmly. "You boys stay right here until Dan gets back. Do you hear?"

"We will," the boys chorused. "But there ain't much to do here. Except shoot marbles."

With an anxious glance at the three boys, Beth closed the kitchen door behind her against the stifling heat and followed Dan and Dorie down the street.

Chapter 10

Walking on wooden legs to the Methodist church where the wounded were being taken, Beth was filled with a suffocating sense of dread. Everywhere houses smoldered as flames licked blackened rafters, although some were already reduced to piles of sullen gray ashes. Down the street lay nothing but devastation, and Beth shivered in spite of the heat.

She felt uneasy about leaving the boys alone, but Dan had promised to go back and check on them later. He marched ahead now, determined and stalwart, and she followed him stiffly, Dorie behind her. She could barely recognize the streets.

"Oh . . ." Dorie panted behind her. "This — this doesn't even *look* like Lawrence!" she moaned. Then she touched Beth's shoulder. "If you don't mind, I'll stop at our house and see how Mother is. She could be worried about me, but she was in such shock about my f-father when I left, I doubt she'll even know I've been gone. I'll catch up with you later," she added as she hurried away.

"Please don't feel you have to come back to help. With all the horror . . . it's hard to know . . ." Beth paused in mid-sentence.

Dan swung around. "Be careful while crossing the street near the church with all the hot ashes blowing around!" He took Beth's arm. "Where's Dorie? I thought she was coming with us."

"She wanted to check on her mother, and said she might come later. I told her not to come if her mother needed her."

Pa and one of the men were carrying a man with a horribly burnt torso as they crossed the street near the church. Beth choked at the pitiful sight and a sense of helplessness swept over her. Dan helped carry another victim into the church.

Just ahead Beth saw bodies lying inert and unmoving on the streets, and her mouth grew dry. Stepping inside the church, she heard the screams of the wounded who had already been brought in. Along the pews lay men who clutched at their bellies where dried blood had already glued their tattered clothes to gaping wounds, and she gasped in horror. Death — and pain — everywhere! Already the church was full of women carrying basins of water, bending over writhing, moaning bodies.

The church swam with the sound of

milling feet of doctors and aides and the groans of men on the pews. Flies and gnats hovered in droning, singing swarms, tormenting the suffering men.

Beth stumbled, her feet unsteady in the filthy aisles, looking for a familiar face. Pastor Cordley poured water into basins from pails standing behind him for the women who had come to assist the doctors. His face was set and strained, and she grimaced. She must help in spite of the horror.

"Beth! I'm glad to see you!" he said as he spied her. "Your father has been a great help bringing in the wounded and the — dead to the place used as a morgue. Here, take this basin of water to Dr. Reynolds, please."

In the oppressive heat she carried the basin toward the doctor — one of the few in the town. She heard screams from a man with a shattered arm lying on the pew where the doctor had snipped off the bloody shirt, and she turned away, trying not to vomit as she saw the scalpel cut into the flesh. Perspiration soaked her dress as the doctor plunged reddened sponges into the water she had brought.

Everywhere Beth could see was blood and dirty towels, and always there were the groans, curses and screams of pain as more men were brought into the church. The odor of sweat, blood, unwashed bodies and excrement rose up in waves of blistering heat until the stench sent her staggering behind the church, where she heaved up her food. Leaning against the stone wall, she braced herself and drew a slow, deep breath. *Some nurse you are,* she scolded herself. So this is what the guerrillas had brought upon the town: the evidence of one man's hatred of its people! How horrible!

Then she marched back into the church. *I won't keel under again,* she vowed when she saw the sick, helpless sense of suffering on the tense, white faces that stared vaguely at her, some with unseeing eyes.

When she returned to Dr. Reynolds, she had calmed herself — at least, outwardly. "I'm — ready to assist you now, doctor," she faltered as she stood beside him once more.

For hours she handed swabs of toweling to him and squeezed bloody sponges in the basin of water for him. She hadn't seen Dan — or her father — since she came in, so immersed was she in trying to help.

Suddenly she felt a light tap on her arm and looked up. Lynn Nelson, his green eyes dull with exhaustion in his drawn face, managed a grin for her.

"Beth — you've been so faithful, helping us here! The devastation is awful everywhere. So many killed — around 150, if we've counted right. Probably more. At least they believe Captain Lane has escaped. He was one of the first persons on Quantrill's list. The man hated him."

"But why? What did Captain Lane do to him?"

"He was the leader of the free-state army." Lynn shrugged.

Just then someone shouted, "Here comes Jim Lane now!" And a weak cheer filled the dim church as the captain staggered in, his haggard face beaming under a scraggly beard.

"You got away from the guerrillas?" Pastor Cordley asked quietly.

"Yes. But barely. It was nip-and-tuck."

"What happened?"

"Well — the noise awoke me early this morning. Immediately I figured what was happening so I dashed outside — in my nightshirt."

"Bet it was a-flappin' round your legs like crazy," someone joshed.

"Maybe so. But all I wanted was to get away. First, I tore my nameplate from the door so they wouldn't know where we lived. Knowing William Clark Quantrill, I figured he hated me most of all. I wasn't about to let him catch me, if I could help it. So I took out toward the cornfield behind the house and

ran over the hill as fast as I could. I —
stopped at the first house I came to beyond
the cornfield and asked for some clothes.
The shirt and pants were quite ill-fitting,
but I stepped into those floppy pants as
quick as I could, asked for a horse — any old
plow horse — and down the road I clat-
tered, warning the people. When the guerrillas found out where I lived, my wife told
them I was gone, so they set the house on
fire, thinking I was hiding inside."

"Your house was almost new, wasn't it?"

"Sure it was. My wife begged them to save
her piano but they were so drunk and un-
gainly they let it all burn. She did manage to
save a few things although the house and
most of its contents burned. They didn't kill
the women but robbed them and the children and burned almost every structure
they entered."

"It's amazing you escaped, Captain,"
Pastor Cordley said.

"Yes, it is, and I'm sure you were prayin'
for me." Then he paused and squared his
shoulders. "But we're going after them. I realize many good men have been killed or
wounded, and the ones who're left are
young boys. But we'll welcome anyone who
wants to help!"

Lynn turned to Beth. "You've already

helped so much today. No wonder you're tired." He placed a consoling arm around her shoulders and looked into her face.

Beth turned slightly and said, "I'd be happy if you went back to the house to check on the boys."

At precisely that moment Dan stepped up behind Beth. "I see you won't need me!" he said abruptly and glared at Lynn. *Is he jealous?* she wondered.

She looked at Dan, her eyes tired. "Oh, Dan, are you going to go fight with Captain Lane?"

"Would — would it matter that much to you?" he muttered gruffly. Then he threw back his shoulders. "After all the devastation I've seen, I must help bring them to justice."

Beth nodded slightly. The air in the church was stifling and suddenly the church began to spin. Lynn steadied her.

"You're about to faint, young lady," Dr. Reynolds said. "Let someone take you home. I sent your father back earlier. He was exhausted too."

"But I — came to help —"

"You can come back after you've rested. Now get on home, Beth!"

"Go ahead, Beth," Lynn put in. "I'll help Dr. Reynolds for awhile."

She stumbled a little as she tried to walk. Dan grabbed her arm, frowning at Lynn as she moved away from the assistant pastor's supporting arm. "Beth-dear . . . don't hurry," Dan chided. "We've plenty of time. At least —"

She looked at him. Her eyes were hooded and troubled. "I guess I'm more tired than I thought," she sighed. "But with all the heat — and the — the wounded. I worry about Andy —"

"I know. At least your father should be with the boys by now. I saw him when I was on the way back to check on them, and he said he'd go instead."

They stepped cautiously across the street and walked together in silence. She lifted troubled eyes and looked into Dan's face.

"Do you think Lane's men will catch up with Quantrill's band? They're so vicious in their fighting!"

Dan frowned. "I'm not sure what we'll find. You aren't concerned for me, are you, Beth? You have Lynn around —" His voice was bitter and she shook her head fiercely.

"Oh, Dan, don't be so touchy! Lynn's my friend, the same as you are. Why should we quarrel?"

"Are we quarreling?" he asked stiffly. "I didn't mean to be quarrelsome."

There was the strong smell of burning wood, much stronger than when she had left, as they rounded the corner and neared the house. Beth stopped and sniffed. "Dan, what's happening?"

Picking up the full skirts of her gray poplin, she ran to the back door where the smell of smoke seemed even stronger.

"Pa?" she screamed. "Andy! Where are you?"

Dan stepped ahead and opened the door. "Mr. Davis? Where are you?" Just then they heard excited voices coming from the chicken coop as her father and brother stepped out, looking filthy and grim.

"Pa, what's wrong?" Beth cried. "Something's horribly wrong. Please tell me —"

Pa moved forward and placed a hand on Beth's arm. "It's all right now, Beth. But —"

"But what, Pa?"

"Quantrill was here, wasn't he?" Dan said with irritation.

"Yes — but all's fine now."

Andy came toward them, his brown eyes wide. "We were up a tree shootin' our slingshots."

"Slingshots? What in the world for?" Dan asked sharply.

"Quantrill really come to torch our place, Beth. He said he had a score to settle with my sister! But Donnie and Karl and me, we sneaked outdoors and climbed up that elm. We was scared to death — but we kept a-poppin' off our slingshots like they was guns! One of Quantrill's men lit a fire by the side door, but the three of us kept shootin' our slingshots so fast they got riled up and turned around and skedaddled away!"

"Weren't you scared you'd be killed?" Beth said, her legs shaking.

"We didn't think they'd shoot us little fellows, so we kept on aggervatin' them until they left. We had quite a time gettin' the fire out, though. It was burnin' on the back side, but we managed to get it all doused.

"That's when Quantrill told his invaders to get outta town. He said his scouts on Mount Oread seen Unionists comin', so they better get movin', and they was off a-runnin'."

"Pa — how long was this before you got home?" Beth's voice was trembling.

Mr. Davis leaned wearily against the chicken coop. "The boys had the fire out and things under control when I got back. We were just checkin' the rest of our property to make sure we didn't miss anythin' when you came."

"And all without a gun!" Beth groaned.

"Well, we did have our bean shooters,"

Karl Howell muttered.

"Talk about gumption!" Dan chuckled. "These boys really showed their courage!" Then he paused. "It's about time for me to go if I want to catch up with Lane."

He tipped his hat, bowed to Beth and started down the street. She watched his swinging arms as he walked away. A sudden pain like a knife-thrust hit Beth's stomach. *Dan is leaving and he hasn't told me goodbye. . . .* Had she made him angry, the way she'd gone on about Lynn? What if she never saw Dan again?

Chapter 11

In the early evening Beth awoke from a restless sleep. Visions of the horror she had seen earlier that day haunted her late afternoon dreams.

Startled by a sound, she rolled out of bed and went into the hall. Pa, his face haggard and gray, stumbled in from the porch.

"Oh, Pa!" Beth cried, hugging him tightly, "Where have you been? I thought Andy went with you!"

He wiped his face with a grimy handkerchief and shook his head. "I — I helped Editor Speer look for his boys."

"Where are they?"

"The youngest boy is alive. He's at home with Mrs. Speer. Junior was shot by a raider on a horse. Seventeen-year-old Robbie is nowhere to be found."

He looked desolately at Beth and his head sagged. "Speer won't believe Robbie is gone! He just keeps callin', 'Please help me find my boy. They've killed him!' "

Just then Beth was startled by a sharp rap on the door. It was Pastor Cordley. "The fires are still glowing in the cellars," he said quietly. "The brick and stone walls are still standing but look like hell itself! John Speer . . ." Pastor Cordley's voice broke. "He's still looking for Robbie."

Beth grabbed his sleeve. "Oh, pastor — we don't know where Andy is either!"

"I thought I saw him earlier with Dan Wilcox."

"Where is Dan now?" her voice cracked. The pastor shook his head jadedly.

"He was going with Jim Lane to bring Quantrill to justice."

"Do you know what shape the town is in?" Pa asked with a frown.

"Only two stores are standing on Massachusetts Street, and all else — the hardware store, the bowling saloon, the bakery, Fillmore's Dry Goods, the Lawrence Bank — is in ruins."

"I think the residential area is a bit better," Pa added, "especially those here in West Lawrence. There was no wind, which helped. Most brick and stone buildings seem to have survived." He shook his head wearily. "It's awful, almost like an earthquake. Almost nothing worth saving is left."

Pastor Cordley passed a shaking hand over his grimy face. "I'd better go. There's so much to do — people to talk to . . ." He turned to the door. "Don't worry too much about Andy. Quantrill's men were ordered not to kill children, you know. God has His hand on His own."

Bless Andy. He and the Howell boys took on the rebels who tried to burn the house. If only I had stayed at home instead of going to the church to help with the wounded! She chided herself again.

Beth sank into a chair, exhausted, and turned haunted eyes on Pa. "It's — getting late. Oh, Pa, when I think of Andy roaming in all that —" she waved her hand helplessly toward the window. "Dear Lord, where is Andy?" she groaned.

Pa sat quietly and bowed his head. She knew he was praying. Silently she joined him. *All I can do,* she agonized, *is to leave him in God's hands. . . .*

Dogs began to howl all over town, and she went out on the porch. For miles around a vast angry glow shrouded the town. She thought of John Speer, searching for his son.

Wearily she returned to the house. Pa had lain down on his bed only to toss and turn, and Beth took the lamp and opened the cupboard door in the kitchen, searching for food. *Andy will be hungry,* she consoled herself, although the thought of food almost nauseated her. Rummaging through the shelves she found a few apples and opened a tea towel wrapped around a loaf of bread. If only she knew where Andy was!

Then she lay down on her bed, but not to sleep. When daylight came she would hunt the streets until she found her young brother.

"Dan —" she murmured drowsily. Did he know where Andy had gone?

Troubled and weary, her tired eyes blinked, trying to keep awake. She knew that many friends had lost everything, and she remembered the stores of potatoes and beets that Andy had heaped in piles in the cellar earlier. *We'll share with those who have no food,* she thought. *We're fortunate the rebels didn't succeed in burning our house.* Protected by bean shooters! She found herself smiling a bit.

Suddenly a long, piercing scream rang out, and Beth sat up quickly. The horrible nightmare wasn't over, although Quantrill's band had left. It wouldn't be over for a long, long time. In the residential section where they lived, the devastation wasn't as terrible. Although dozens of homes had been torched, many had been saved by brave women with pails of water.

When morning finally dawned, Beth fixed a pot of coffee for Pa and set a basket of rolls

113

on the table. He staggered into the kitchen and sat down at the table. He looked haggard and weary as though he'd had a sleepless night.

"I slept for an hour or so," he murmured darkly. "But in the long night hours I talked to the heavenly Father. He assured me that Andy was all right. I'll try to find him."

"Let me go with you, Pa," Beth said quickly, but he shook his graying head. "Please stay here, Beth. If you're here when he comes back it will mean much to him."

She paused, then nodded. "Maybe Pastor Cordley has found him. Or — or Dan."

Dan Wilcox. He had often irritated Beth, being so cocksure about himself and his relationship with her. She knew Dan had cared for Andy, but she hadn't wanted Dan to be a part of *her* life.

After Pa had left, Beth stirred up a batch of bread dough. She knew people who had lost everything would need food, and it would be her duty to help feed them.

The town itself seemed dead. No sound of the usual clatter of horses and wagons or the bustle of conveyances. The street seemed black and still, except for the red glow of coals where a house had once stood.

There was nothing left with which to buy food for those who'd lost everything, and very little money remained. Of the three banks in town, two were robbed of every cent, and the third spared because the vault could not be opened. And more victims were discovered almost every hour.

Beth heard the sound of hoof beats and glanced out the window. Dan Wilcox? He was to have joined Jim Lane. Why was he here? He slid from his horse, rapped briefly and let himself into the kitchen.

"Beth? You here? I met your father searching for Andy."

"Dan! Has Pa found — ?"

"No, not yet. But Andy's been with the Howell boys, so your father is at their house now." Dan looked at Beth with a searching gaze. "Get any rest? You look exhausted." He took the chair she offered him. "I've been concerned about Mr. Speer. He was hunting for his second son."

Beth sighed. "Have they found Robbie?"

Dan shook his head gravely.

Beth drew a deep, ragged breath. "Dan — what will happen to Lawrence now? Do you think the citizens will rebuild? Or be afraid to try?"

"People aren't talking. There's a lot of fear. Some of the raiders have threatened they would return to finish the job by leveling the town."

"Oh, Dan! That would be awful!"

"But Lawrence citizens aren't folding their hands, I hear. They say that this morning travelers, emigrants, teamsters and curiosity seekers have jammed the roads and are now streaming into town. But any newcomer is looked upon with suspicion. Any proslavery man is quickly surrounded by an angry mob."

Dan helped himself to a cup of Beth's coffee and the slice of warm bread she shoved toward him.

"Bodies are still being carried to the Methodist church," he added as he set down the empty cup. "Already many bodies are swollen, and the stench downtown is awful, they say. Identifying victims now so they can bury the dead is what's on the minds of the townsfolk. Most carpenters were killed or their tools stolen. Without coffins, they're making rough caskets for burials."

Dan got up and started for the door. "Let me see if I can find your brother." He smiled wryly and started for the door. "I promised Jim Lane I'd be back. We want to see Quantrill brought to justice." Stooping lightly, he kissed Beth softly on her lips, then went through the doorway.

A great feeling of sadness and sorrow overwhelmed her as she thought that many of the town's citizens were to be buried in one massive grave. And she nearly wept over Dan's lingering kiss. Was this a "goodbye" forever?

Beth kept glancing though the window to look for Pa's tired figure, but the street lay idle, with only the weary citizens plodding stolidly toward the Methodist church to continue to identify the bodies and make burial plans.

With a shake of her head Beth went back into the kitchen. *I might as well clean up the smoke stains where the rebels tried to burn down our house,* she thought as she got a bucket of soapy water.

At least it gave her something else to think about. She prayed for Pa and Andy and for the many broken hearts on this Saturday afternoon. Her hands shook as she scrubbed the smoked-up walls and wiped the grimy streaks from the wainscoting.

Today was Saturday, a day she normally would make sure Pa's good shirt was freshly ironed and Andy's shoes shined for Sunday. But today — *Dear God, what an inglorious day,* she thought. The hideous job of searching for corpses, for half-roasted bodies could go on for hours — hours that stretched beyond forever. . . .

Chapter 12

Early Sunday morning Beth opened her eyes,
tired from worry and loss of sleep, as the sun-
beams pried through the windows. She had finally slept, after committing Andy into the
Lord's hands again. Now she prayed — not
only for her young brother, but also for the
searching men, many of whom had raked up
charred bones from the embers or the dead
bodies found sprawled among the weeds and
gardens. She moaned at the thought.

The human loss was as unfathomable as
the material loss was irreparable. Beth
couldn't get up from her knees as long as the
endless list of needy friends and citizens
streamed through her mind. She knew
Pastor Cordley had planned a funeral service for the townsfolk at the church, and she
wanted to dress as simply and reverently as
possible. When she got up, she pulled a
clean blue figured gingham dress with its
simple round lace-edged collar from the
closet and slipped it over her head. She
shuddered at the news Pa had brought when
he finally dragged himself into the house

after the exhausting job of helping bring the bodies to the Methodist church. When the church was full, bodies were taken to other churches, he said. She knew that through the day and into the night the heartbreaking thud of shovels had echoed through town. At the cemetery atop Mount Oread a crowd had moved quietly, reverently, in the dim arc of lamplight as boxes were lowered into makeshift graves throughout most of the night.

Now work was set aside while a few citizens gathered for Sunday morning worship, although the usual joyousness of song and praise was missing.

Pa had returned to his work of preparing the dead for burial. Beth tied on her bonnet and headed for the Congregational church. Women and children gathered there, dirty and wearing wrinkled and bloodstained clothes. The horror and anguish of the past two days had taken their toll.

Slowly they shuffled into the rough pews, sad-faced and teary-eyed, and slumped down, looking expectantly into the tired, lined face of Pastor Cordley who stood before them, his Bible opened to Psalms. The service would be short and simple.

He cleared his throat and began to read softly: "The Lord has spoken to us all in these past few days," he said in words that faltered slightly. "Psalm 79:1–3 says: 'O God, the heathen are come into thine inheritance; thy holy temple have they defiled; they have laid Jerusalem on heaps. The dead bodies of thy servants have they given to be meat unto the fowls of the heaven, the flesh of thy saints unto the beasts of the earth. Their blood have they shed like water round about Jerusalem; and there was none to bury them.' " His voice broke, and everyone was silent. Then they swallowed their sobs as he continued: "But God — is among us, and He won't leave us. Please remember that!" The sound of weeping in the small clusters of women grew stronger.

Then the congregation returned to the task of preparing the bodies of their loved ones for burial. Beth walked soberly among them, placing consoling arms around those she knew had lost husbands or fathers especially, and spoke a few words of comfort or offered dry corners of her handkerchief to wipe their eyes.

"Thank you, Beth . . ." a few whispered, burying their faces on her shoulder. "God bless you. . . ." *I don't know what I can do,* she thought, *but maybe offering a shoulder for their tears will help.* Her own tears began to fall, and her thoughts turned again to Andy. She asked a few people if they had seen him, but no reply gave her hope.

The heat accelerated the decaying of bodies, and the stench became unbearable. Before the day was done, ceremony was deserted and many of the bloating corpses — except those whose families buried their loved ones in backyards — were lowered into one common grave.

Beth closed her eyes and clenched her fists as the stiff bodies were thrust heavily into the makeshift grave. How could she ever forget this day?

Leavenworth sent aid in the form of food, clothes and other supplies. Visitors continued to stream into town, some to help and others only to stare. Many were newspaper correspondents and illustrators who began sketching and recording eyewitness stories.

Most accounts came from those who had managed to escape. But as the journalists wrote, one thing stood out clearly: the raw courage and grit of the women.

Early estimates placed the damage in the town at millions of dollars. Nearly every business and merchant had lost everything.

"But we still own our properties," Beth overheard a hopeful murmur. "And we can always rebuild." Drooping spirits seemed to lift a little.

Beth joined a cluster of disheveled women on the east side of the church who shared an event that had happened just before Quantrill and his band left town: "Him and his rebels came out on the Whitney House porch," said a tall, skinny woman, dabbing at her eyes as she spoke. "Quantrill turned around and stared at us weepin' women and the burnin' town and got on his horse. He swept off his hat and said with a bow, 'Ladies, I now bid you good mornin'. I hope when we meet again it will be under more favorable circumstances.' Then he turned and rode out of town. The beast!" she spat out.

Someone muttered harshly, "Some raiders actually said they was comin' back to finish the job!"

Beth shook her head and started for home. *Surely the raiders are out of Lawrence for good,* Beth grimaced. She fanned her hot face with her bonnet as she hurried down the street. The house would be stifling, she knew. She stepped on the porch and opened the door, and she thought she heard a noise.

"Beth? Is that you?"

Andy's voice!

"Andy!" She shrieked as she stumbled into the kitchen. There he sat, his bare feet in a pan of water.

"I felt dirty and figured I'd better get washed up." His voice was nonchalant.

"Andy —" Her voice was stuck in her throat. She wanted to scold him for being disobedient, but all she could do was reach out and hug him. She was so thankful she couldn't speak.

"I know I shouldn't use one of your good towels," he said apologetically, "but that's all I could find."

"Oh, Andy . . . Where were you? Where have you been?" she grabbed him and hugged him again. "Pa and I have been so worried!"

"Well, ya know I'm nine and can take care of myself!"

"But Andy — there were hundreds of evil men in town creating a lot of havoc! You've been gone all day Saturday and today, and you didn't think we'd worry about you?"

He splayed his bare wet feet on the floor. "Ya see, it was like this, Beth. I was down by the Howells', and the boys and me, we was a-walkin' when we seen the ol' Liberty Pole. It was standin' straight and tall by the river's edge, ya know. Karl and Donnic and me — we decided it was up to us to save it from that wicked Quantrill bunch. That's where we was — until this mornin'. Didn't anybody tell ya?"

123

"How could they? Pa was looking for you and I was at the funeral this morning. You haven't had anything to eat, have you?"

"Well, remember Lydia Stone from the City Hotel? She brought food and drinks to the wounded and she gave us somethin' to eat."

"But why didn't you let Pa or me know where you were?"

Andy picked up a pair of gray-knit socks. "Oh — I guess we didn't think —" He looked up at Beth with a bright smile. "And we did perteck that Liberty Pole. We overheard some of the raiders say, 'They're just a couple of pipsqueaks.' Ain't that somethin'?"

Beth knew that the Liberty Pole near the river was still there. Though she couldn't condone his disobedience, she also couldn't destroy Andy's conviction that he had helped. And now the terror was over. They were safe.

The odor of charcoal and embers was strong in the air, but the wind turned. It brought a cool breeze that seemed to sweep away the horror of the past few days. It was as though there was nothing more to fear. Beth thought of the burial of the more than 150 men she had witnessed. Now she hoped the town could put the horrible scene behind them and start over.

Suddenly Beth heard yelling. She ran to the window just in time to see a rider dash by, his long hair streaming in the wind. As he galloped down the street, he bellowed, "They're coming again, they're coming again! Run for your lives!"

As Beth glanced wildly around she caught a glimpse of flame in the dim distance to the west and the scream froze in her throat.

Someone was already ringing the Liberty Armory Bell, and soon there was a mad stampede, for few wanted to face the second wave of horror the town had experienced so recently. Men, women and children — all rushed blindly, filling the streets with a bedlam of sobs, shrieks and shouts, as though Quantrill himself was on their heels. When the dust settled, there was only dead silence.

Beth's heart hammered in fear as she pulled Andy into her arms. *Dear God, what's happening? Is Quantrill back? Will Pa be safe? Oh God* . . . She dropped to her knees in fear and prayed.

Then a shrill voice shouted, "It's all right! A farmer just burnt a field of straw!"

Chapter 13

Beth breathed a shaky sigh of relief. They were safe. "Andy," she spoke quietly as she touched his shoulder, "the town is in shambles in the business district, and many have lost everything. Pastor Cordley gave a very meaningful message as he conducted the funeral. But there's so much need! Let's cook up soup to feed those who are destitute."

"Look at the sky," Andy said, pointing to the west. "It's still reddish from the embers! What do you s'pose will happen next? Will Quantrill actually come back as he said he would? The threats is what's scary. Can we —"

"Can we trust the bushwhackers to stay away?" Beth picked up the thread of conversation. "That's where we must trust God. It's like someone said, 'We still have our property.' If the town rebuilds, the people will have homes again. Yet it will take a lot of courage and work. Some homes are still intact, especially those built of stone and brick. Now it's up to us to take scrub buckets and clean up smoke and grime of those we can."

"Yeah. We kin help out with the smoke and grime, all right," Andy said with a sigh. "Got plenty of rags, Beth?"

That night was a vicious summer night: Thunder shook the house and lightning lit up the sky. Hail and rain pattered relentlessly against the windows, and hurriedly Beth closed them against the storm. In the midst of the fury Pa stomped into the house, his clothes soaked from the icy wind.

He pulled off his wet shirt and washed his muddy hands. Beth eyed him sharply. "How are things going downtown? What did the town leaders decide to do? Will the raiders come back as they threatened?"

"We hope we've found all those who've been massacred," he said solemnly. "But praise God, we've been safe this time around too. When I think of all the sorrowful faces of women and children, then of the scare by that burnin' hayfield, it makes me angry! Andy?" He called out sharply. "Did he get home all right?"

Beth nodded. "This afternoon when I came into the house he was here, calmly washing his feet!"

"I looked for him, then was drafted to help prepare the dead for burial. Someone said they'd seen him with the Howell boys. I figgered the Lord would keep him safe. Sometimes we must just trust. I hope you scolded him," Pa added, stifling a little raspy cough.

"I couldn't scold him. After all, he was doing his part to protect the Liberty Pole with the Howell boys! He's usually sensible, you know."

"Well, he did prove himself to be trustworthy." Pa paused, rubbing his chin. Then he went on. "I noticed that the Miller block of business places is burnt. Most was burned, some valued at $1 or $2 million, I hear. How many were killed, I wonder?"

"I heard that there were 150 or more, and about 80 women widowed. Someone said that over 200 children are without fathers," Beth said sadly. "It's so heartbreaking! Luckily doctors from Leavenworth came to help patch up the wounded. Maybe —" She paused, then added, "maybe it's good that Dan Wilcox went to join Jim Lane's army to go after Quantrill." She shuddered. "If only the militia would help Jim Lane. But knowing Jim Lane —" she faltered.

A day or so following "Black Friday," as the day of horror came to be called, Governor Thomas Carney took steps to what he hoped would prevent another massacre and to pursue Quantrill and his band. For the next issue of *The Leavenworth Daily Conservative* he ran this notice:

Col. C. R. Jennison — Sir, the State of Kansas has been invaded. To meet the invasion you are authorized to raise all the effective men you can. I call upon all loyal Kansans to aid you. Kansas must be protected at all costs! The people of Leavenworth and every county in the state will rally to avenge the lawless sacking of Lawrence and punish the invaders.

Your ob't servant,
Thos. Carney, Governor

Beth pored over the contents of the paper, hoping to find facts to ground some of the rumors that were flying. Several men in Lawrence were accused of spying and were to be dealt with harshly, the paper said. John Calloo was tried after the raid. Calloo obviously had advance notice of the forthcoming raid and had moved his family out of town quietly. The man Taylor, whom Pa had met at the Eldridge House, had been a spy.

Rumors soon grew rampant, and Beth dreaded to open the next issue of the *Con-*

servative. But there it was — Calloo was convicted and was to be hanged. Beth was almost overwhelmed with the horror that had wreaked havoc in town.

"I understand the Cates family left town too," Pa said a day or so later when he came home. Some others also had packed their belongings and left, he said. *Whom can we trust now?* Beth thought bitterly.

To cover her sorrow she and Andy donned old clothes and scrubbed smoke-stained walls and charred furniture of homes that still stood. The sickening odor of burnt flesh still clung over the low areas of town. There was so much to do, so many homes to scrub.

Governor Carney, not long after, wrote another article for the paper: "Lawrence is in ashes. Thousands of acres of property have been destroyed, and worse yet, nearly 200 lives of our best citizens have been sacrificed. No fiends in human shape could have acted with more savage barbarity than did Quantrill and his band in their last successful raid!"

Even *The New York Times* reported on the catastrophe: "Quantrill's massacre is almost enough to curdle the blood with horror. In the history of the war thus far . . . there has been no such diabolical work as this indiscriminate slaughter of peaceful villagers. It is a calamity of the most heartrending kind — an atrocity of unparalleled character!"

Soon newspapers all over the nation blazed with such grim news. People were sickened and stunned after reading about the atrocities. No other acts of violence had approached the Lawrence butchery. How could this have happened?

"Beth, you oughtn't get all grimy and gritty, cleaning up our house," Mrs. Fox told her as she saw the filthy water in Beth's bucket.

"Why not?" Beth said. "The least we can do is help homes that are still standing."

She watched as Beth sponged the gray, dismal kitchen. "Mmm. What do you hear from Dan Wilcox?" Mrs. Fox prodded. "He was once sweet on you, wasn't he?"

"He — joined Captain Lane's brigade. That's all I know," Beth said quietly.

The news came that Brigadier General Thomas Ewing and several hundred cavalrymen armed with repeating rifles had joined the chase while Quantrill rushed his raiders across the state line into the safety of Missouri, and Beth bristled at the thought. It was said that Quantrill had admitted smugly that his most remarkable raid was the devastation of Lawrence.

People were ready for revenge.

Revenge! No wonder small groups of Union pursuers went on a rampage in Missouri, of burning and killing.

Four days later General Ewing issued Order No. 11, which decreed that within days all persons residing on the border counties between Missouri and the Osage River must leave the land. Rebels living in the towns occupied by troops were to be expelled. The few loyal Unionists who lived in the countryside could move to military posts or any part of Kansas beyond the border. All grain and hay, either stored or growing in fields, were to be burned.

Hearing and reading this accumulation of dubious news, the weary citizens of Lawrence continued steadily to work on rebuilding the town, their faces grim as they worked.

Beth had not heard anything of Dan in weeks. Was he still with Jim Lane? She was a bit uneasy, knowing Captain Lane's reputation of ruthlessly pushing his men.

Food continued to arrive from the country. Supplies from Leavenworth still poured in. Some of the badly wounded had died, and funerals continued. Wherever she could, Beth brought fresh vegetables to homes where she discovered limited food supplies.

Reports poured into town. Leavenworth had subscribed $15,000 and continued to raise more. Governor Carney opened his own pockets and chipped in another $1,000. The state and the nation came to the aid of the beleaguered town.

In spite of all the donations, a feeling of sadness permeated the town. How could they ever rebuild the smoking ruins? It looked hopeless.

When Captain Lane and his bedraggled men rode into town a few days later without the stolen animals and other properties he had promised to return when he set out, discouragement wiped out the small degree of hope that had momentarily surfaced.

Beth grew even more strict with Andy and his roaming around town. "I want you to stay here and not get into any more trouble," she snapped when he begged to go with the Howell boys to the ravine.

"But Beth, I —" he whimpered.

"I know you're trying to be responsible, but when I see so many homes who've lost loved ones, I'm so thankful you're safe. Let's keep it that way. We can't take any chances."

"Well, the bushwhackers weren't supposed to kill children anyway," Andy muttered. "I'd been safer than you realize. And the Liberty Pole —"

She gave Andy a quick hug. "You see why I was worried, can't you? I'd hoped I could trust you!"

Andy nodded and sat down on the back porch. Beth shook her head. She hoped she'd gotten through to him this time. She'd have to do something to make it up to him later.

Just then there was a shout as the two Howell boys leaped across the shallow ditch. Because Beth knew the pair were rambunctious and fun for her brother, she shook her head again and went out to greet them.

Donnie doffed his hat and swaggered toward Beth and Andy. "I guess Lane's really gonna go after the Missourians, to hear him talk. Boy, wouldn't I like to join that army and go with 'em. Jim Lane said —"

Beth waved Donnie to stop. "We've known Jim Lane for a long time. He's been something of a scoundrel in the past. We — don't always trust him very much, even though he means well."

"Well, where's Dan Wilcox? What does Dan say?"

Yes, where is Dan, now that Lane's men are back? Beth wondered for the hundredth time.

Donnie Howell squatted on the porch. "Jim Lane bragged a lot about what he'd done while he was a army captain. He claims him and his men killed at least fifty of Quantrill's bushwhackers and wounded lots more."

"Yeah, then their 'maginations really flew," Karl went on. "Some claimed they'd killed over 800 guerrillas. You believe that?"

Beth smiled a little. "Does anyone? If you believed anything Jim Lane said, few, if any raiders would've made it to Missouri alive."

"We've heard his tales for years," Pa said, coming up the walk. "People just aren't impressed by much he says anymore. I guess folks are more concerned about those fresh mounds of sod." He paused and covered the cough that almost strangled his words.

"What will come of it all?" Beth murmured, pushing aside the window curtains when she came into the house. In the semi-darkness she saw several figures dashing through the dim streets. *What's going on?* she wondered.

No one had mentioned Dan Wilcox. Where was Dan now? A bitter taste settled in her mouth. Had she been too quick to turn against the farmer who had proclaimed his love for her?

Chapter 14

Daylight came, slow and gloomy. As Beth awoke, she got up and went to the window and looked out. To the south the trail wandered, black against the cold gray of the damp morning just as the sun edged up over the rim of the horizon in the east. In the distance cottonwood trunks stood out white and naked against the dark arches of low green hills.

She moved to the cookstove and raked the dead embers, throwing in a handful of kindling. Soon a small fire blazed and she set the water kettle on to boil for coffee.

In the distance Beth heard the harsh sound of hammers pounding to rebuild what had recently been black, charred rafters of a house down the street. A feeling of dejection swept over her. She shook herself mentally. *I will not be gloomy*, she vowed.

Beth busied herself in the kitchen, cooking a potful of chicken soup, thick with great wedges of carrots and turnips. Then she pulled on her faded blue sunbonnet and left the house. Everything was soft and quiet in midmorning sunshine. She had earlier given Andy permission to play with the Howell boys — provided they stayed on the narrow road south of town that led toward Mount Oread.

"Be sure to mind Mrs. Howell," Beth ordered her brother sharply. "And do what you can to help clean up the burnt homes."

Carrying her kettle of soup, Beth started down the street. Everywhere the odor of burnt wood and charred ashes lingered. Would this acrid smell stay with them forever? As she walked along she was aware of activity: men and women bustling about, hands and faces blackened as they tackled the grime. She noticed the scrawny woman bent over a washtub outside a badly charred kitchen. The woman looked haggard and troubled as she hung the few tattered skirts and blouses on the line.

"Good morning!" Beth said cheerfully, setting down her soup kettle. "Do you need help? I brought over some soup for you. It seems your kitchen's about done for."

"Don't bother me," the woman muttered sullenly. "I'm tryin' to wash up these few rags I found. It's about all I got left. But after —" She paused and shook her wispy head. "You're Miz Davis, ain't you? I can't understand why God 'lowed them bushwhackers to do this horrible thing to our town!"

"Did you lose anyone in the massacre?" Beth ventured hesitantly.

"You might say I did. I found — my — husbin's skull, after someone helped me rake through the rubble 'n' ashes."

Beth nodded. She vaguely remembered hearing about a woman who had found her husband's skull — Mrs. Maines, wasn't it? Wasn't she one Pa had tried to help?

"I'm sorry about all the trouble this town has suffered. I thought perhaps you needed something to eat, so I brought over this soup. In spite of all the furor, God still loves us. And He won't forget us. And He won't forsake us either. He promised —"

"But I still don't know why God let it happen," the woman cut in. "Why did He let Quantrill's band come into town and do this to us? It's them Missourians! God coulda stopped 'em."

"I'm sure I don't know what His reasons were. But if we can hang on —"

"Why should we trust a God who leaves us when we need Him most? Does that seem like He loves us?"

"But He knows what's best for us. We can't understand His ways —" She stopped and drew a deep breath. "The Bible says,

'When thou passest through the waters, I will be with thee; and through the rivers, they shall not overflow thee: when thou walkest through the fire . . .' "

"That's exactly what I done! I'd tried to hurry my husbin' to our cave," the woman snapped. "But I was too late. When when I found his skull I hugged it to my breast. All I had left of him! And it was all the Missourians' fault!"

A chill hit Beth as she recalled the long, piercing scream heard throughout the town in the wee hours of Saturday morning; this was the woman who had been found among the gutted buildings; the woman who said she had feared her husband had been shot the day before. After searching through the scattered remains of ashes she had found . . .

A shudder passed over Beth. Here was this strange, scrawny woman trying to pick up the pieces of her life by washing the few pitiful tattered garments she owned. *And I dared preach to her*, Beth thought, biting her lip sharply.

"I should'a done like the woman next door," Mrs. Maines said blandly. "She fooled the rebels by burnin' oily rags and made them think it was her home that was in flames."

How awful! Beth shook her head fiercely.

Who would avenge this terrible travesty? It was one thing to blame Quantrill's men, but another to attack innocent people in Missouri. She knew that a lot of anger and fury had already boiled up among the poor, beleaguered citizens at the devastation. No wonder Mrs. Maines seemed deeply troubled. People were only too eager to destroy as they had been destroyed.

Beth wondered how Pastor Cordley felt about all this violent fervor. She'd heard Senator Lane had already stirred up flames of fury night after night with his fiery speeches. The "wicked Missourians" should be punished, he'd vowed.

And there was the rivalry between General Thomas Ewing and General John Schofield, she'd heard. It was Schofield, the West Pointer, whom President Lincoln had asked to take over the Kansas militia. He had hoped Governor Carney would check the frenzied move to invade Missouri across the border. Schofield strongly opposed the wholesale slaughter of the people across the border. He finally took on himself all the authority vested in him by Commander in Chief Abraham Lincoln. Beth wondered how things would work out. Who would take over the army?

For Pastor Cordley a week of funeral services continued as bodies were discovered almost daily. Beth knew he sometimes fell asleep outside the battered homes while waiting for rites to begin.

Slowly she started for home, her mind in turmoil. People like Mrs. Maines not only needed physical comfort but the comfort of God's Word.

The church had been designated as a depot for clothes brought in from surrounding towns. There was so much to do, so much pain to ease, Beth discovered. Where did one start?

When she stepped into the kitchen door, Pa was sprawled by the open window reading *The Leavenworth Daily Times*.

He cleared his throat. He was hoarse. "Listen to this, Beth. The editor's warnin' the people. He says, 'The storm cloud that now hangs so bleak and threatenin' fury over the ill-fated border must be guided with a wise and iron hand, or it will burst upon us, involvin' all in one ruin.' And that 'iron hand' sure ain't Jim Lane!" A small cough scratched from his throat.

Beth set down her empty soup pot and eased herself wearily into a kitchen chair. "Well, what does it mean, Pa?" She noticed his drawn face, his troubled eyes. "Schofield? Thomas Ewing?"

"God willin', not another one of Lane's meetin's. We ain't gettin' much work done, with Lane callin' town meetin's every night. What Lawrence oughta do is get busy and rebuild the town into a mighty city. But the call to vengeance grows constantly stronger."

"Pa, do you really expect this to become one of the biggest towns in Kansas?" Beth asked. "Dan Wilcox seems to think that someday we may even have a university here, but that's worlds away."

Pa drew a long, deep sigh. "Someone's already donated land toward that, I hear. With folks like Peter Ridenour from R & B's Grocery still in town I guess almost anythin' can happen. Did you know he's already set up shop behind the rear of his gutted corncrib as soon as the embers was out and is still sellin' salt? Somehow his credit ratin' is still good. He even flies the American flag atop of it. He's leavin' the Missourians out of it. That's what I call gumption and guts!"

"But it will take time to rebuild —"

"We've got all the time in the world. That reminds me: I'd better get back to the mill and see what needs fixin' there." He got slowly to his feet with a ragged cough and started for the door.

How tired he looks, Beth thought. *He's truly given himself to the whole town in the way he's helped with burials and searching for wounded. And now with fixing up* . . . she sighed. God only knew how much strength Ben Davis had sacrificed to Lawrence. There'd been so much to do and he had wholly thrown himself into it.

Chapter 15

On August 27, with militia patrolling the outskirts of the town, Jim Lane and men of like mind held a rally at Leavenworth's Mansion House. News of James Lane and his plans to punish Missouri had dribbled into that town with every ferry crossing.

The senator himself, drawing crowds with little effort, muttered and harangued his fellow Kansans. "Think of ridin' down the street, and seein' 150 of your fellow citizens cooked on the sidewalk!" he burst out angrily.

Pa decided he should be there too. After all, it concerned the town of Lawrence. Beth shook her head. *He ought to be in bed.*

In all of Kansas history there had never been a larger, more unruly crowd. Mayor Anthony, Charles Jennison, George Hoyt and other well-known radicals regaled the people, calling for the destruction of Western Missouri. It was exactly as Mrs. Maines had responded.

Lane, prancing in their midst, clenched his fists as, in a frenzy, he bellowed: "Extermination — I repeat here that for self-preservation, there should be an extermination of the first tier of Missourians until we are secure!" Uproarious cheering followed.

"What was Schofield doin' while fiends were murdering the citizens of Lawrence? He was taking oaths of allegiance to their companies in Missouri. I take the ground of *vengeance,* if blood and devastation are needed for safety. . . ."

No wonder thunderous cheers followed for what seemed to be the cry for revenge, to scorch Missouri black with fire! They had set the date for September 8. Soon they would settle the problems on the border in one sweep of a wholesale slaughter in Missouri!

Mayors, senators and congressmen apparently stomped hardest for it; prominent radicals and editors everywhere seemed to glory in the idea of revenge. After all, wasn't it a band of Missourians who had devastated Lawrence only a few short days ago? To punish Missouri at any cost seemed to be the only answer.

When Pa staggered into the house after his day at work, he flung his gray hat into one corner of the kitchen floor and shook his head angrily.

"It ain't right! I understand General Schofield can put a stop to this ungodly action!" he told Beth and Andy when he came home. "Revenge belongeth to the Lord. This must be kept out of Jim Lane's hands! Most people know if they follow Jim Lane they're actually goin' the wrong way. But I know there's some clear-thinkin' people who're beginnin' to realize this. I hope to God Schofield can stop this senseless slaughter before it begins!" He covered his faded blue eyes as a look of utter sadness lined his face.

Then, stifling a cough, he struggled to his feet without his usual pause for evening devotions. With only a weak "good night" he shuffled into the bedroom. Beth watched him go. She knew he'd been in a turmoil of helping with activities ever since the day of the massacre. First assisting with carrying the wounded into the church, then helping carry more and more bodies to prepare for burial. And then digging the trenches for the mass burial . . .

And yet there was still so much left to do. Homes were slowly being rebuilt, then a few more had cleared away the debris to begin rebuilding. But it had been a tough, painful process. No wonder Pa was as tired as he was, being in the midst of it all.

146

Fortunately, a few stalwart citizens like Peter Ridenour had worked hard to start things moving again, and Beth knew Pa wanted to help. But he was simply exhausted. She decided he must stay in bed and recuperate, and she went to bed with a heavy heart.

On the morning of the planned invasion, Pa staggered out the door in spite of threatening skies and Beth's protests. Big drops of rain splashed down on muddy streets and winds shrieked and blew. In spite of Lane's embittered speeches, a small crowd had gathered around Lane's podium. His ranting and raging continued in the deluge for three hours. Yet enthusiasm for the planned invasion seemed to be waning. Thinking quickly, Lane shifted his speeches to slavery, Schofield and Quantrill.

"Why in the world don't Schofield go after him then — if he can't catch him, why don't he let us go?"

"Yeah, let's go get Missouri!" shouted someone in the crowd.

"But Schofield won't let us go!" Lane shouted. "He wants to let them raiders go free!"

With that, the meeting closed and the men splashed home listlessly. Obviously a good number could see the truth of the matter — that this was the end of the border war.

Coughing heavily, Pa dragged himself to bed that night after he'd told Beth hoarsely what had happened. He failed to get up when the sun broke through the clouds in the morning. Beth waited wearily at his bedroom door, but when her father didn't come out, she listened and heard his labored breathing. She ate a lonely breakfast. Andy had eaten a hearty meal of creamy oatmeal and slammed down his empty glass.

"Please, Andy, be quiet," she shushed her young brother. "Do check the chicken coop to see if the hens have survived the heavy rains. Then clean the nests and make sure they have fresh straw."

"Uh — do you s'pose Lane left last night with his followers?" he asked as he spread jam on a thick slice of bread.

"I don't know. But rumors will continue. They claim Quantrill himself has issued an edict, requiring all Union citizens south of the Kansas River to be off the land in fifteen days. Well, don't worry, Andy. No armed bodies of men will be permitted under any pretext whatsoever to pass from one state to the other!" She kept her voice low, listening to sounds from Pa's bedroom.

At a sharp rap on the kitchen door, Beth went to open it. Had Dan finally returned?

"Hello!" Dorie called out. "I haven't seen you since the day of the massacre. How have you been, Beth?"

Beth hurried to her friend and hugged her tightly, then pulled out a chair for her. "Oh, Dorie. It's been so long since I've seen you — since your father — since Edward —" She choked back a sob. "How have you and your mother survived?"

Dorie took off her bonnet and twisted it in her hands. "I didn't come because I felt it best to stay with Mother. She — she's taking all this much better than I ever dreamed. But —"

"But about Edward — ?"

"No one has seen a hair of him. Oh, why did Quantrill have to be so cruel?"

"And some people trusted him," Beth said quietly. "We didn't believe he'd invade our town! He's wrecked so many lives."

"Yes." Dorie caught a sob in her throat.

"Pa's — been out helping. Now he's exhausted and may be sick. If we didn't have the Lord —" Beth whispered.

"He's what keeps me going. But you've been feeding so many people and helping clean up. You've worked hard."

A small silence settled between them.

Then Dorie ventured, "What — what do you hear from Dan Wilcox? Was he still with the militia?"

Beth's face fell. "I — haven't heard from him."

"Do you feel any different about him, Beth?"

"At first I didn't know how I felt about him. He — he didn't seem to follow the Lord, but — but he's a decent person, Dorie. I turned away from him. And now I don't hear from him at all! I just don't know —"

"If you hear from Dan, I hope you won't turn him away. Or do you love Lynn Nelson?"

Beth jerked her head toward Dorie at her abrupt question. She paused slightly, then she shook her head. "No — no, I don't think so. But he's everything in the church Dan is not. A strong believer, a firm Christian with a concern for spiritual things." Beth tapped her fingers on her lap. Dorie got to her feet and pulled on her bonnet.

"Well, I'd better go. Mother and I — we manage the best we can. At least Quantrill didn't burn down her house!" Tears ran down her cheeks and she wiped them away. "I hope your father gets better." Dorie hurried out of the house.

Just then the bedroom door creaked and

Pa staggered from the door, hanging shakily on to the lamp table. Beth jumped to her feet, her eyes wide. His face was ashen and he burst into another fit of coughing.

Suddenly he stumbled to his knees and collapsed.

"Pa . . ." Beth screamed and rushed toward him. What was happening to her father?

Chapter 16

Beth reached her father and caught him just as he fell.

"Dorie! Help!" she cried. But Dorie had already left the house without hearing Beth's plea.

She eased him gently to a chair where he broke into another paroxysm of coughing. Pa had been soaked from the recent rains, and he'd obviously been overtired with all the work he'd done.

Just then Andy burst through the door, and Beth raised one hand in caution.

"It's Pa!" she cried. "He — he's caught a bad cold."

Andy drew back, his face troubled. He must have read her deep concern in her eyes, for he was at her side instantly.

Pa's usually tanned face was pale. Always so strong and stalwart, he had seemed invincible. But now . . .

"I — I guess I caught . . . a bit of . . . cold," he sputtered. "When — I got so wet and — and then attendin' Lane's meetin's . . ."

"You should've stayed home as I begged you!"

Beth touched his forehead and noticed how hot it felt. Andy eyed him anxiously.

"Lemme fix up your bed nice and warm with hot bricks while Beth stirs up somethin' hot for you to drink, Pa. Then you'd better go to bed."

"But — but all the — the work . . ." Pa burst into another fit of coughing.

"Don't worry. We'll take over till you feel better," Beth said. She turned and went into the kitchen and fixed some hot milk laced generously with honey. Andy darted outside and brought in several bricks he found near the chicken coop. He laid them in the oven, heated them and lugged them into the bedroom. Then he gently unlaced Pa's boots and pulled them off.

After Pa had gulped down the hot milk, Beth and Andy helped him into bed. Beth covered him up, carefully arranging the hot bricks as comfortably near his feet as she could. Then she bent over and kissed him. "Now take a good long nap, Pa. After you wake up you'll feel better. I know Mama always believed in 'sleeping off' a cold."

She motioned to Andy and they quietly left the bedroom. Then she sank into a kitchen chair and laid her head on her arms as the minutes ticked by.

"Oh, Andy," she whispered, "I'm afraid Pa's awfully sick! What can we do?"

He straddled a chair and leaned his arms on the back. "Do ya know what Mama used to do for lung fever? It's been so long I don't remember."

"L-lung fever?" Beth echoed. She jerked up her head. Had Pa's bad cold already turned into pneumonia? "She — cut onions into thin slices and sprinkled sugar between each layer and let them stand for an hour, then she made a poultice, I think. That's all I remember."

"Do we have onions in the cellar?"

She shrugged. "I used some for the grouse last time Pa shot some, but — I don't remember how Mama made a poultice!"

"Well, keep Pa good and warm." Andy placed his hands behind his back. "I'll bring in more firewood so you can try to fix some onion in the oven."

Should she really keep the heat in the stove when it was so hot already? Yet keeping the stove hot and using plenty of covers tickled Beth's memory as one of Mama's "remedies."

Andy picked up the wood basket and hurried out the back door while Beth tiptoed into Pa's bedroom and felt his forehead. It was still as hot as fire.

If "sleeping off" a cold had worked in the past, it wasn't working on the Kansas plains in the heat of summer. The house was growing hotter than ever. Pa tossed and turned all afternoon, moaning and coughing until Beth despaired of being able to bring him relief.

Pa had the dreaded "lung fever" that had taken its toll of babies and grown-ups every winter on the prairies. She knew it got into the chest and set it aflame until one could no longer breathe.

Perhaps she could cool his forehead with cold cloths. She hurried into the kitchen where Andy was stoking the fire.

"Wind's dyin' down," he muttered. "I'll do Pa's chores and go after some milk. Hope our little pile of wood will last awhile."

Beth nodded, taking several towels and plunging them into a pan of cool water. "Why don't you see if Dr. Reynolds can come out? You know where he lives, don't you?"

"Sure do. I'll hurry," Andy said, jamming on his cap. "Don't ya worry. Just look after Pa. I'll bring in more firewood." With a slam of the kitchen door he was gone.

Beth wrung out the towels and walked softly into the bedroom. Pa's face was flushed and damp with sweat. He looked so pale, so drawn. Carefully she patted the wet towel on his face.

"Our dear, wonderful Pa," she whispered, "please, please don't leave us! We need you. Please get better!"

Amid praying and chafing his hands between her own, she tried to rouse him, but there was no response.

A few minutes later she heard Andy slam the kitchen door and she flew to meet him as he threw down more stove wood.

"Andy, Andy," she cried, "he — he doesn't say anything. He's very, very sick. Please — please hurry out to Dr. Reynolds as fast as you can."

"I'll be back soon. Keep them bricks hot. And —" he fumbled in his pocket, "here's a bottle of patent medicine I found in the shed. Pa told me once it was real strong but good for a cold. I'm off now." He whirled around and rushed out of the house.

Beth watched as he dashed down the blackened walks. Then she picked up the bottle of medicine, poured a cup half full and stirred in a generous dose of honey and carried it into the bedroom.

Pa had flung off his covers and his glazed eyes seemed vaguely lucid. She knelt down and pushed the cup gently to his lips.

"Please, Pa," she said softly, "please drink this. Maybe it will help. I — used some of the patent medicine Andy said you'd saved for colds. He's gone for the doctor."

Pa choked and flung the cup onto the floor, where it shattered. "Beth —" his voice was slurred. "So hot — in here . . ."

What do I do now? she thought wildly. She hurried to make another cold towel compress, trying to cool his feverish brow and shoulders in a continual cycle of wringing towels and changing compresses.

She glanced at the clock. If the doctor would only hurry!

Pa began to cough again and Beth bent over and stroked his forehead. It was so hot, and she threw his covers back. *When will his fever break?*

Just then she thought she heard a noise outside. Andy and Dr. Reynolds! She jumped up and rushed through the kitchen and flung open the door. Andy was alone.

"Doctor — couldn't come," he panted. "Out on another call."

Beth's heart sank. *God, where are You?*

Chapter 17

From somewhere a thought came to her: "Thou wilt keep him in perfect peace, whose mind is stayed on thee: because he trusteth in thee."

Beth dropped to her knees. Why had she not thought to ask the Great Physician what she should do?

"Andy," she said, "pray with me. We'll have to trust God to help us through this."

Andy nodded, his freckles contrasting against his pale face as he knelt beside her.

"Dear God," Beth began, "I've never been so scared in my life! You've kept our pa while he helped others, so please help him now," she whispered raggedly. "Please, please, tell us what we should do for him!" She poured out her fears and pleas.

After several minutes she stood and gave Andy a shaky smile. She had remembered what to do for an onion poultice. What else? Should she keep the stove hot? The heat of the day was almost smothering them as it was . . .

"Well," she told her brother, "let's start

what we remember. We'll slice a panful of onions to bake for poultice."

The kitchen soon grew redolent with the strong scent of onions as Andy peeled and Beth chopped and sliced, all the while trying to remember what else her mother had used for remedies. Suddenly a thought came to her: *wild mustard for a plaster.* Of course! And hot goose grease!

"Quick, Andy," she urged, "go see if there's still some goose grease in the cellar. I think we just have to heat it up and then we can rub it on Pa's chest. It's supposed to warm a person through to his lungs, if I remember right. And bring some wild mustard, too."

With only a moment's hesitation, Andy scampered off. Biting her lip, Beth placed the panful of onions and sugar into the oven. *Dear Father, thank You for the ideas. Oh, I hope this works!*

Within minutes the hot goose grease was melted enough to spread. Woodenly Beth picked up the pot and went to the bedroom. She knelt beside Pa as he coughed a few times and tried to push her away.

"Pa, we want to help you!" she begged, tears cutting shiny paths down her cheeks. "Please lie still!"

He was soaked with sweat, tossing and

turning, thrashing wildly whenever she tried to place her hands on his chest.

"Pa — please!" she cried. Andy moved silently beside her.

"Please, Pa," he said solemnly, his voice shaking a little, "let us help you. I don't know if Beth and me can live here in this burnt-up town by ourselves. You gotta let us help."

As Pa sensed what they wanted, his flailing arms grew still. His face looked so haggard, so sallow, that fear clutched Beth's heart again. *Is Pa still alive?*

"Go check on the onions, please, Andy," Beth murmured. She suddenly felt very weak, and she didn't want Andy to see. Tears spilling from her eyes, Beth rubbed the ragged throat, the chest that now rattled with phlegm, praying silently as she worked. At times his breath came so fast and hoarse that it sounded like a whistle.

"I put them onions into a bag, Beth," Andy said, trying very hard to sound grown-up. "Now we just gotta put it on his chest." He did so with great dignity.

Beth's heart thumped with fear at the tense look on Pa's withered face. "Maybe . . . we should let him rest now," Beth whispered. "I think I remember how to make a mustard plaster in case this doesn't work." *Thank You for that memory, Father,* she prayed.

Rummaging through tins on the kitchen shelf, Beth took down some lard.

"Beth," Andy's voice began tremulously behind her, "what would we do without Pa? He's always taken care of us. He brought us to Kansas from Massachusetts and all —"

Beth turned and took both her brother's hands in her own. "The Lord knows what we need, Andy. Do you think I'm remembering what to do for Pa on my own? If He is faithful in these little things, He'll be faithful in the big ones — like taking care of us, no matter what happens."

Andy nodded. "But Beth, why did He let Quantrill burn down our town? Why did He let so many people die?"

"I don't know, Andy," Beth managed, fighting back tears again. "The Bible says His ways aren't always our ways. He told Job that a long, long time ago. I guess it's hard for me to understand too. I don't know why God took our mama away when we were so young. Do you remember the funeral? The pastor said that no matter what, God was still with us, and that He had a plan for our lives. That God will carry out His plan — in His own time."

Andy sat down at the table. "I guess you're right, Beth. It's just scary, that's all."

"I know," Beth sighed. "Let's keep busy and take our minds off what might happen. Now for the mustard plaster . . ." *Dear God, help me do this right!*

"You use hog lard?" Andy asked incredulously.

"Yes," Beth said with confidence she didn't feel. "We just take two tablespoons of hog lard and a spoonful of ground mustard and mix it."

An hour later Pa still lay white and feverish, and Beth shook her head. "I think it's time for the mustard plaster, Andy." But fear gripped her throat. "We'll just find some flannel to smooth it onto . . ."

"We don't have any flannel, Beth."

"Well, I know just how to remedy that," Beth replied, keeping her voice light. Going into her room, she selected a warm petticoat, and with a brisk tug she had ripped a suitable piece off for the plaster. Andy gazed at her wide-eyed as she smoothed the lard and mustard onto the fabric.

Pa lay with his eyes closed, but the wheezing in his chest had almost stopped. Beth placed the mustard plaster on the thin chest and leaned over to kiss him. He looked so pitiful. "Whatever is best, Lord. Help us to accept it . . ." her voice choked as she whispered.

Night came, and Beth and Andy were silent, both exhausted as they sat at the kitchen table. But as night drew closer to morning and no sound came from Pa's bedroom, Beth threw herself on her knees beside his bed and clasped one of his hands in hers.

She must have fallen asleep on her knees when she felt someone shaking her shoulders.

"Beth, honey, I think you better wake up."

Opening her eyes wide, she stared at Pa's face in the feeble light of the lamp and blinked. His hands felt quite cool; and his eyes were wide open. He grinned weakly with a congenial smile. She threw her arms around him and hugged him hard.

"Oh, Pa — Pa, you're going to be all right, aren't you?" she cried.

"Couldn't leave — you and Andy — quite yet, could I?" he said in a hoarse voice. "Andy's been such a handful and needs us b-both!"

Beth began to cry with great sobs of joy and relief, tears that dripped over Pa's sheet. *Thank You, Father. Thank You.*

Chapter 18

The days passed slowly — mid-September days with morning chill and daytime warmth, touched with the scent of coming autumn. The peculiar Midwest aroma of loam and subsoil, dust, corn and apple trees lingered in the air. Already the constant charred odor of burnt wood was dissipating.

Pa was up, pacing restlessly through the house. It was all Beth could do to keep him lying down to rest.

"Pa, you *must* get your strength back," she scolded. "There's no need for you to be up because there's really nothing for you to do!"

"But there's still so much to do — homes still needin' to be rebuilt and finished. I feel I'm no good any more." Roaming restlessly through the house, he puttered around straightening pictures on the walls, moving furniture. Plainly he was bored.

Shaking her head, Beth sent Andy to get Dr. Reynolds in desperation. If Pa wouldn't mind her, maybe he'd listen to the doctor.

Some minutes later the doctor arrived, his

neatly trimmed black beard showing signs of gray, his small hands tucked in his pockets.

"So you've been sick," the congenial little doctor said as he checked Pa's pulse and scrutinized his haggard face carefully. "You certainly overdid yourself getting all your neighbors back in shape. Then getting soaked in the rain, worrying about Lane's next move — well, you've done just too much! I'm ordering you to rest for another week, and I don't want any arguments! There are still so many disheartened folks around. Once you roam around town they'll ask you to do this or that. I won't have it!"

"But I could talk sense into some of them," Pa fumed. "There's no sense in feelin' hopeless, like some still seem to be."

"You're absolutely right, Mr. Davis. But you're simply not ready to take on anymore difficulties. And there's still a lot of talk. Every time the breeze shifts, another rumor starts up. Some are sure that Quantrill's still coming — murdering and pillaging, wanting to move to kill and burn everything and everyone. Some terrified families have streamed to larger towns or gone back to wherever they came from, and people are still out of their minds with fear! You have no business to get mixed up with them. Get

165

yourself back in good health first."

Pa buried his head in his hands. "But if I could help them — set them straight —"

"No!" The doctor's words were firm. "For now that's not your job. Please calm down."

After the doctor left, Pa seemed to have grown quieter, but he pummeled Beth and Andy with countless questions.

"Is it true that Lawrence has dug trenches, pits and breastworks to protect the town? Why wasn't I told about it?"

Beth looked at Andy and sighed. "Well, it seems there's still fear everywhere. Most able-bodied men have joined the militia led by General Schofield. Why weren't you told? Because you'd insist on being out there!"

"Yeah, that's where I'd be, if I was only old enough!" Andy burst out.

Scouts ranged the countryside, patrolling the Santa Fe Road from the Missouri border west as far as Council Grove.

"We might as well build a wall around Kansas!" Andy snorted.

"Well, tell Pa what's happening downtown these days!" Beth prodded. "The blackened shops and stores are springing up again. Even the new bridge across the river is making progress. Help has come in from all over. There are still many good people around."

Pa was silent; he stroked his beard gently and Beth could see the hope stirring in his face. "Then who's gettin' them stirred up to rebuild?" he said lamely.

"We're trusting God never to let this happen again," Beth answered quietly. "Most men here have gone off to work each morning with a musket or revolver under their coats, and Lawrence citizens are ready to fight. We'll be back on the map again, Pa. You'll see!"

A knock sounded on the door. As Beth hurried to open it, Pastor Cordley's tired figure slumped in.

He fumbled with his cap in his hands. "I hear that Brother Davis has been very ill, but with all the sick people in Lawrence I've had my hands full as I've tried to cheer them up. With all the rumors of Quantrill and his band that filter in — well, that's easy to understand. People are just full of fear — instead of trusting the Lord."

Beth pulled up a chair facing Pa and motioned him into it. "You might try to cheer up this man too! He bemoans the fact that he can't get out and help. Dr. Reynolds has given him strict orders to take care of himself until he's recovered."

"It — it's been hard to think of all the cleanin' up and fixin' up in town — and I'm not able to help," Pa muttered.

"You've worked yourself half to death as it is," Pastor Cordley said kindly. "But the Lord has used you in a mighty way. You've been a great help!" Then he turned to Beth. "Has Lynn been here lately?"

Beth jerked up her head sharply. "Lynn Nelson? No, not recently. Of course —"

"What of Dan Wilcox? Have you heard anything from him?"

Beth shook her head slowly. "Not a word. I — I'm not sure if . . . I know Lynn needs help with Bible studies especially when school begins and there are sure to be Bible classes. I feel my first job is to see that Pa gets well."

"Yes, of course." He nodded. "But as soon as you can, I'm sure Lynn will want you to assist with Bible teaching."

Pastor Cordley shifted his legs and sighed. "The rumors are still flying. Quantrill and his roaming around. The news now is that he's heading south. But no one knows where the blow will fall!"

A mild, warm breeze blew through the open window and the scrim curtains dallied gently. Beth's mind turned again to Dan. There'd been no more word of him. Why

168

hadn't he gotten in touch with her and let her know where he was? It puzzled her. She remembered the times he had told her he loved her, but that had been long ago. And he'd gone to fight the men who were with Quantrill. Now there was Lynn Nelson, looking for her to help him in the work of the church . . .

Pastor Cordley slowly struggled to his feet and shook Pa's hand. "I pray you'll recover quickly, Brother Davis. Somehow — some way, the Lord still has work for you — after you're well."

Pa stretched his long legs. "One way or another, He'll find something for me. But it's hard to trust."

"It is for all of us! But we know God will care for His own. We have so many prayers running up to heaven," Cordley said. "Well, I must go. Keep up your courage. We'll see you out again one of these days."

With that he shut the door.

Chapter 19

Fall had fully arrived. The sounds of saw and hammer resounded through the quiet streets as homes rose where once had been blackened skeletons. The air was chill but mists were rising, and a long band of rich, warm light lay over the sloping spur of the bend of the river where it fused with the blue morning shadows.

The aroma of new lumber and sawdust grew heady. The houses weren't the same as before the fire, and the stooping little town was haunted by the absence of the men who had left to track down the cruel band who had tried to wipe it out. But the town was gradually returning back to life.

Pa had gone out to see what progress was being made, and Beth followed him. He walked slowly, pausing to speak to the men still suspicious of any stranger who meandered through the streets. She was on her way to the church to meet with Lynn, for she had promised to help with Bible studies on the following Wednesday night. Rumors still ran rampant like a Kansas whirlwind.

The plan was to press the guerrillas so vigorously, so relentlessly, that flight would be their only option. The townspeople hoped to flush out those who hid toward the south on the prairie beyond.

"If we could only catch that demon . . ." The words still re-echoed between hammer blows. "With so many border fighters now on his trail his total escape is hardly possible!"

"We need more men like Dan Wilcox," one of the dusty-streaked men muttered as Pa and Beth paused to watch the men pounding nails on one of the homes. "If he hadn't been hit —"

"What do you mean?" Beth gasped to one of the workers who had served under Schofield.

"Oh, he was one of General Schofield's best men — till he was wounded."

"Wounded!" she cried. "Do you know where he is now?"

The man pushed back his dusty felt hat. "Nope. But I served with him, and believe me, he fought hard. That's about the time General Ewing stepped up Order No. 11."

Pa leaned against the skeleton of the house that was being raised day by day. "Just what does that mean?" he asked quietly.

"As far as we can see, it will lead to still

fiercer and more active fighting, but it will put an end to the border war. All men are determined to keep Quantrill out of Kansas, no matter what the cost. But some say —" the man paused.

"Say what?" Pa said, his voice hard. "What do you mean?"

The man sighed. "If Quantrill *wants* to come back, the general feelin' is that nothin' can keep him outta Kansas."

Beth spun around and headed for the church. That wasn't what she wanted to hear. And if Dan was wounded — or killed . . . Her heart lurched. Would he ever come back?

She hurried down the street until she reached the stone church. The front door stood open and she stepped inside.

Someone was seated on one of the pews, rustling the pages of a Bible.

"Beth!" Lynn turned quickly and sprang to his feet. "I was sure you were coming to help me. In fact, I've been waiting for you to come."

Beth managed a weak smile. It was hard to think of teaching materials when Dan . . . "What if we plan on a group of youngsters for our first Bible study this fall?" Lynn continued enthusiastically. "We need to focus on a verse that would speak to them. I was thinking of Isaiah 43 — you know, 'Fear not: for I have redeemed thee, I have called thee by thy name; thou art mine. When thou passest through the waters, I will be with thee; and through the rivers, they shall not overflow thee.' "

"That's what I think we should stress, Lynn. So many have been filled with fears, and they don't understand it. How can we tie this in with God's love?"

" 'When thou walkest through the fire, thou shalt not be burned; neither shall the flame kindle upon thee,' " he continued. "I see what you mean, Beth. Do you have any ideas how we can approach this?"

Beth was silent for several seconds. "I remember how troubled Mrs. Maines was about it all. I tried to get her to understand, but I came up blank. I'd still like to find the answer for her — even though she didn't understand."

"That's very compassionate of you, Beth." Lynn paused, and took her hands in his. "Beth — Beth, do you know something? You're so wise, so capable. After all this furor is over and we can start life over, will you do me the honor of marrying me? We'd work so well together. You know the Bible and you could be such a help to me."

She withdrew her hands. Marry Lynn

Nelson? But — no, she couldn't think about that. At least, not yet.

"Lynn — I'm not ready to think of marriage. Somehow —"

"You're still thinking of Dan Wilcox, are you? I know he seemed very fond of you some time ago, but he — he hasn't shown up for so long."

Beth pressed her lips together firmly. "He left to go after Quantrill. Did you know that the rumor is that he's been wounded? I — I can't think clearly, Lynn. I'm not even sure how I feel about him right now. But until I know —"

Lynn stepped backward, and she saw a troubled look cross his face. Her heart went out to him. After all, Dan hadn't given her a sure word of his relationship with the Lord. He'd seemed so distant toward God.

A somber darkness seemed to have fallen over the afternoon as she started toward the door. *Oh, Lord, what shall I do? What's the right answer?*

She stepped from the door and started down the path. A rabbit bolted in front of her, and she lifted her gaze toward the sky. The sun had left its smoldering fire in the west and was gone from sight. A rich sacrament of color flowed from the sloping hills into the deep chalices of the valley.

As she made her way slowly down the path, she heard Lynn's words after her. "I'll be waiting for you," he said softly, and Beth hurried toward home.

Chapter 20

Late November had blown cold and damp, the previous day's light snowfall leaving the streets raw and muddy. The whiteness had gone, but everything lay sodden under the cold, heavy air. As the iris-blue of the sky slowly widened, the day dawned, and thin pink sunlight filtered through the clouds, glistening on uneven wads of fog below.

Beth drew her shawl around her shoulders and started for the church. Those who were spared from the massacre had talked to the pastors about a Thanksgiving time to praise and thank God, and Pastor Cordley had agreed to it.

The service would be held at the Plymouth Congregational Church because it was roomy. Elizabeth Fisher had promised to help Beth with the dinner plans.

"After all, we've managed thus far," Mrs. Fisher told Beth when the two met on the muddy path on the way to church. "Many of us have repaired our homes, and although much still needs to be done, we're making progress. We've lived in our barn all these weeks. Hugh has worked hard on getting the insides of our house finished. Luckily it was brick on the outside."

"Yes. I hope the townsfolk will take time out for this praise service. I'll fix a huge pot of potatoes, and we still have plenty of carrots and onions."

"But why shouldn't they come?" Elizabeth Fisher, her dark hair parted in the middle, beamed brightly. "Do you mean that not everyone will have extra food to bring? I'm sure there will be enough. Hugh went hunting early this morning and shot two wild turkeys."

"How nice!" Beth exclaimed. "I see Lynn has built a fire in the stove and the church will be warm as we make our plans. Yes, Lawrence has been through some horrible times this summer. I know many have lost much more than we have, but to share our food and thank our God for His tender mercies —" Beth paused.

Mrs. Fisher stepped up to the door and opened it. "You're right, although I'm not sure everyone feels that way, after losing husbands and fathers. I'm so glad Hugh was spared ... hiding under the house — in that little hole of a cellar — even though I had to use my wits to keep those guerrillas from finding him."

"Did you really wrap him in a rug?"

"Oh, yes! I thought sure they'd burn our house to the ground!" she choked out as she stepped into the warmth of the sanctuary.

"We'll need to cart in some planks for tables," Beth said, surveying the church. "But tell me, how did you roll him in the rug?"

"I was determined to save our kitchen — as long as Hugh was under the house, you know. I — even drenched my dress with water, waded through the flames, then flooded the kitchen floor, since Hugh lay under it. My neighbor Mrs. Shugre dashed over and asked why I was trying to save the floor while my world was burning. I yelled, 'I want to save our land!' above the roar of the fire. That's when I told Hugh he must crawl out secretly from under the house, although I think he was almost roasted by then. When he crept out I threw a dress over him, and as I lifted the carpet he ducked under it."

She sighed and shook her head. "I dragged the carpet across the yard until I was all out of breath — and I dropped it beside a weeping willow tree. My neighbor helped me grab some chairs, bedding and other stuff and we piled it all over the rug. Then we put my little Joseph on top of the heap, and we watched and prayed so the rebels wouldn't suspect Hugh was under it!"

"Didn't the youngsters give him away?"

Elizabeth smiled wanly. "Joseph heard him speak. His voice was hoarse, asking for water. He said, 'Pa's under here somewhere. I heard him — talk.' I shushed him and told him to be quiet."

"And no one suspected your husband was safe," Beth murmured as she checked the stove and closed the damper.

"God's grace was marvelous! I told Mrs. Shugre in a loud voice, 'Let's throw those chairs on top of the carpet.' I told little Joseph to go to the stable and get a rake. By then I was shaking like a leaf! I kept Hugh under that pile of stuff until about 11 o'clock. By then all the raiders had left."

Beth drew a deep breath. Here was another brave woman who had dared to save her husband in spite of grave difficulties. It was incredible how the Lord had spared thirty to forty people.

When their plans for the Thanksgiving dinner were finished, Beth took Elizabeth's arm and headed for the door. "We'll ask Lynn to be in charge of the planks for the tables. I hope we'll have enough food for our feast," Beth said pensively. "We planted some pumpkin seeds in the patch behind the chicken coop last spring and raised a good crop. I'll bake pies for the dinner."

"That's gracious of you, Beth. Somehow we'll find enough food for us all. I'm sure the folks at Leavenworth will pitch in and help."

The two women left the church. Beth's mind was awhirl as Mrs. Fisher told her of other events that had occurred on August 21. The wounded had been moved to the churches after the pews had been taken out. Women, some with babies in their arms, ran through the streets, screaming for husbands and sons. Two doctors, fighting swarms of blowflies, were bending over the wounded. By 4 p.m. Elizabeth was roaming frantically over town searching for her son Edward, fearing he had been killed.

"I walked all over, calling his name," Elizabeth continued. "Freddie Loaman stumbled toward me and told me Edward was alive. So I went back to the house and met Hugh in the garden under a peach tree. He put his arms around me and we praised God quoting Psalm 34:7, 'The angel of the LORD encampeth round about them that fear him, and delivereth them,' I kept saying. 'Has he not said in Psalm 50:15, "Call upon me in the day of trouble: I will deliver thee, and thou shalt glorify me"?' "

Those are words for Mrs. Maines, Beth thought. The two women had reached the corner where Beth turned to skirt the ravine. With a wave of her hand she turned and left.

Her mind whirled with the experiences of which Elizabeth had told her, and she shook her head. It was incredible that 300 armed desperadoes should be able to pass over forty miles of Kansas by night and pounce upon a town like Lawrence at daybreak without warning! And then they marched leisurely back over the same territory with 250 troops following on their heels . . .

Now it was all beyond weeping and wailing. It still seemed too deep and too serious for tears and lamentations. The magnitude of disaster was beyond one's wildest thoughts, even the thoughts of those who were in the midst of it.

These past three months had been hectic ones. Fully half of those who weren't killed were homeless and reduced to short rations. Yet none suffered want. God had been gracious to those whose lives were spared.

"We must put Lawrence back together," people had insisted, and it was happening now. Buildings were built better than before, Beth noticed. All alarms at night had proved to be false. But Missouri was too near to leave Lawrence at ease. Yet, with Thanksgiving so near there was much for which to thank God.

Chapter 21

For the next two days the aroma of pumpkin pies baking in Beth's oven wafted through the kitchen. Her mind was so busy that she had little time for much else. Andy had gone back to school reluctantly a few weeks before, and Pa was still at home, carrying in stove wood and puttering around the yard.

The weather had grown brisk and chill, and the prairies were tinged with frost. Thanksgiving Day dawned bright and clear. Beth layered the big gray kettle with potatoes and strips of creamed turkey and fixed a pot of buttered carrots. Then she changed into a fresh figured print of pale blue, combed her hair carefully into a neat chignon, set off with her mother's tortoiseshell combs.

She hurried to the door and called out, "Andy? I need you to help carry these pies to the church!"

He bounded around the house, patting his stomach, and grinned. "Punkin pies, you said? I been smellin' them all mornin'. You ain't scared I'll snitch one of them before I get there, are ya?"

"Don't you dare!" Beth flared as she handed him a box. "This is a day for thanks, remember. Now please carry them carefully. And don't stumble when you hop across the ditch. Pa?" she called out. "I'll let you carry this kettle of potatoes. Better wear your coat. It's chilly outside."

She slipped into her dark-blue wrap as she picked up the pot of carrots and followed him out of the house. As she set her footsteps toward Vermont Street, she took deep breaths of the vigorous autumn air. Ahead of her Pa carried the kettle. Everywhere she saw people hurrying down the street toward the church, some balancing their food in small pots. Although most people skimped on meals these days after the massacre, she knew the spirit of camaraderie was strong, and anticipating a hearty meal and fellowship would take priority today.

As she scrambled up the path toward the church steps she saw Lynn standing beside the door. He reached for the food Beth carried in her cold hands.

"Here comes the pumpkin pie baker!" he quipped. "Your neighbors breathed the delectable aromas for the past hours, and I'm in on the secret!"

"I hope Andy got them here safely. I think his mouth watered all the way up here!" she laughed.

"They're safely stashed on the end of the long planks you and Mrs. Fisher ordered for the table. It's amazing what foods have come, including some squirrel and baked sweet potatoes."

Beth wrinkled her nose. "Squirrel! Well, I know people brought what they had. Elizabeth and I did our best to spread the word."

"You did a wonderful job." He took her wrap and hung it on a nail beside the door.

She heard a familiar chuckle and turned. "Oh, Mrs. Maines! You did come. I'm so glad you could join us."

The scrawny little woman smiled wanly and clasped Beth's hand. "It was good for you to invite me. I had to scrounge around for somethin' but I had saved the last of the persimmons for somethin' special and fixed a pie."

"Good! I'm sure people will enjoy it." She scurried to the front of the church and surveyed the laden table. Now where had all the food come from? And the stack of tin plates? Had someone else provided them? A murmur of voices and sounds of stifled laughter swept over the background. *I can tell this is a good idea,* she thought. *We need this time of togetherness. After all, we've been through so much together.*

There were no rumors of danger this day, and the crowd seemed calm and relaxed. A sense of love and security hovered over the church. There was much chatter in the background as people related bits of news. With each passing day there was less to remind them of that awful "Black Friday." Stores were prospering, and people had swarmed back into town. Perhaps some remembered that from this very same church had come powerful messages of God's love and grace from Pastor Cordley. The same brushy ravine outside, where the little boys played and chased rabbits, had once been crowded with scores of terrified men who'd tried to hide down its steep slopes. Now all was calm and peaceful.

Pastor Cordley stood before the crowd now, banging a spoon against a plate. "Friends," he called out, "this gathering today is one of celebration for lives which have been spared. Men have died horrible deaths, but God in His wisdom has spared some and showered the women and children with His goodness. Let's sing a few songs of praise before we walk past this table heaped high with God's gracious benevolence on this day of thankfulness. Let's sing

'Come, Ye Thankful People, Come.' "

Lynn started the first song and voices — some cracking with tears — joined in. Sobs choked Beth's throat as she looked around the room. Somehow, it seemed God's love sifted over the crowd. Women, remembering lost husbands, and maidens, thinking of sweethearts, let tears flow freely. Mrs. Maines wept copious tears, and Beth placed her strong arms around the thin, shaking shoulders.

The little woman wiped her eyes with one sleeve of her gray print dress. "You reminded me that God didn't forsake us, and I can see today that He'll keep on lovin' us through each other. You were right. We've needed Him all the time — but didn't realize how much. I trust Pastor Cordley can explain it to me now."

"Just ask him," Beth said softly. "Just ask him."

People began to file past the table, picked up tin plates and heaped them high with food. Beth and Dorie stood nearby and assisted. To Beth it was a very special time, and her eyes misted again.

Lynn came and stood beside her, filling empty plates and pouring coffee. He glanced at her tenderly and smiled. *He's still waiting for his answer,* she thought.

Just then the door opened with a gust of cold air, and a thin, haggard man hobbled inside. Beth's heart lurched. *Dan? Is it really Dan Wilcox — this gaunt man staggering among the crowd?* He seemed almost too weak to stand.

Slowly she walked toward him. "Dan . . . Oh, Dan — you're back!" she cried. "I'd prayed you would. But I didn't know . . ."

Lynn hurried up to Dan and led him to an empty pew. He drew off Dan's battered hat. "Rest while I fix a plate of food for you. You must be hungry." He walked to the table and selected a plate.

Beth sat down, staring at Dan, seeing the shock written all over her face. He shook his head.

"I — I'm not very — hungry," he said hoarsely. "Oh, Beth, my darling, it's been — so long . . ."

"Too long! Oh, Dan — how I've waited . . ." She choked on her words. Then she stumbled on. "But why didn't you let me know you were coming? I'd waited to hear for so long. I'd almost given up —" Her voice trembled. "And when you left without telling me goodbye —"

Dan shook his head wearily. "You — you seemed to be occupied with — with other things —" he nodded toward Lynn. "And then we — tried so desperately to find Quantrill and roamed all over southeast Kansas and Missouri — until we realized he had slipped away. It was horrible. We crossed over to Missouri, for Governor Carney had promised to help us find him. Yet in spite of all the skirmishing he must've escaped. We tried — really tried! But he and his guerrillas had disappeared from the face of the earth, it seemed."

"What happened to you?" Beth asked in a weak voice.

"For so long I hated Quantrill and I wanted only to find him and put a bullet through him. He'd been so vicious, killing so many people. But I kept hearing Pastor Cordley's voice, 'Thou shalt not kill.' I knew Christ had died for the ungodly. And if I was guilty of trying to kill him, I was as bad as he. Then our scouts caught hint of the trail. It seemed Quantrill was retreating east to Missouri. Horses stumbled and fell, men slipped from saddles and were dragged by their stirrups. And always, even in the early mornings, there was heat and suffocating dust. The hunt in Western Missouri continued for days. By then we were in terrible shape. We were aware that he and his band had headed south.

"Suddenly, in mid-September, we were in

a skirmish in Western Missouri. There I was wounded, a bullet in my shoulder, and was hospitalized in the home of some sympathizers who tenderly cared for me. I knew I could no longer fight. But then I — couldn't eat, and I lost my strength. Weeks went by and I decided to walk home. I was given a skinny roan and I began to ride — rode like a maniac. All I wanted was to go home — back to Lawrence. I — wanted to see you." He paused and wiped his eyes. "Beth, I love you so, my darling. And here I am — But I see you with — him." He pointed toward Lynn at the food table. "If you — tell me to leave, I — I'll go. If you're betrothed . . . but I do want you to know that while I was still fighting, I asked the Lord to be my Savior, my Guide. I made sure my faith would carry me — no matter what your answer was . . ."

He half-staggered to his feet, but Beth grabbed his arm and pulled him down beside her again.

"No, Dan. Please sit down! I — must admit that I was tempted to marry Lynn, but somehow I knew suddenly that I loved you. You know, you never really let me know whether you wanted to marry me — except to tell me you loved me . . . but you didn't come back . . . And with Pa being so ill . . . I know you'd have stood by me if you could. I knew I could always count on you!"

Dan's face softened and he slipped his arm around her shoulders. "Beth — Beth, I'm sorry I couldn't let you know I'd changed toward God. I knew that was important to you and it became important to me too."

Lynn returned with a heaping plate in his hand. He stopped abruptly as he saw Dan's arm around Beth and turned stricken eyes to her. "I — I suspected you loved Dan, but I kept hoping you could care for me," he said softly. He put one hand on Dan's shoulder. "But it's all in God's hands. May He bless you both!" Then he turned and headed for the door.

Beth watched Lynn leave the church. He was a good friend, but he wasn't the man for her. She turned to Dan and touched his arm gently, a question in her eyes. "Dan? Once Dorie told me I shouldn't push you away if I ever felt I could truly care for you. After many women lost their true loves, I — didn't want to lose mine too!" She smiled through her tears.

Dan moved slowly and took Beth in both his arms. "Oh, my darling . . ." he whispered in her ear. "By God's grace — I want you with all my heart!" His kiss was soft and gentle on her lips.

The long dark days since August 21 were finally over. Whether Quantrill was gone from Kansas forever didn't matter any more. As the other women of Lawrence were picking up the pieces of their lives, she could do it too.

"Yes, Dan. We'll start over."

The employees of Thorndike Press hope you have enjoyed this Large Print book. All our Large Print titles are designed for easy reading, and all our books are made to last. Other Thorndike Press Large Print books are available at your library, through selected bookstores, or directly from us.

For information about titles, please call:

(800) 223-1244
(800) 223-6121

To share your comments, please write:

Publisher
Thorndike Press
P.O. Box 159
Thorndike, Maine 04986